DEVIL'S PLANET

DEVIL'S PLANET

by

MANLY WADE WELLMAN

RAMBLE HOUSE

2014

CHAPTER I

Water, Water—Nowhere

YOUNG Dillon Stover woke easily and good-humoredly, as usual. He knew he was in bed, of course—but was he? He felt as though he were floating on a fleecy cloud, or something.

He stretched his muscular long legs and arms, yawned and shook his tawny-curled head. He felt light as a feather, even in the first waking moment. He was alert enough to remember now. This was Mars, where he weighed only forty percent of what he weighed at home in the Missouri Ozarks. He'd come here to carry on the scientific labors of his late grandfather, which labors he'd inherited along with old Dr. Stover's snug fortune. For the first time in his life Dillon Stover had fine clothes, independence, money in his belt-pouch—and responsibility.

That responsibility had brought him to Pulambar, Martian City of Pleasure, for study and decision.

He sat up on the edge of his bed, looking around the sleeping room. Its walls were of translucent stuff like ground glass. Upon them, delicate as dim etchings, rippled a living pattern of leaves and blossoms that waved in the wind—a sort of magic-lantern effect from within, he decided. Such leaves and blossoms had once existed on Mars, long ago before the planet began to dry and choke with thirst.

Somebody looked in. It was Buckalew, his grandfather's old friend, to whose care Dr. Stover had entrusted his grandson's Martian wanderings in a posthumous letter of introduction.

Robert Buckalew was a man of ordinary height, slender but well-proportioned, with regular, almost delicate features that seemed never to change expression. Like most society sparks whose figures were not too grotesque, he wore snugly tailored garments and a graceful mantle. He looked very young to have been a friend of Stover's grandfather. His dark hair was ungrayed, his expressionless face unwrinkled. What kind of man was Buckalew? But Dr. Stover had died—suddenly and without indication of the need to die—and his grandson must trust to that letter of introduction.

"Good morning," Buckalew greeted Stover. "Good afternoon, rather, for it's a little past noon. Sleep well?"

Again the young man from Earth stretched, and stood up. He was taller than Buckalew, crawling with muscles. He grinned, very attractively.

"I slept like a drunkard without a conscience," he said. "That flight in from Earth's tiring, isn't it? When did I get here? Midnight? Thanks for taking me over like this." He glanced around. "Am I in some de luxe hotel?"

"You're in my guest room," replied Buckalew. "This is a tower apartment. I'm in what they call the 'Hightower Set', living 'way above town. Come to breakfast."

The meal was served in the parlor, a dome-ceilinged chamber with rosy soft light and metal chairs that were as soft as the bed had been. Or was that more Martian gravity? The servant was a clanking figure of nickeled iron with jointed arms and legs and a bucketlike head with no face except a dimly glowing light bulb. Stover had seen few robots at home on Earth, and he studied this one intently.

"A marvelous servant," he commented to Buckalew as the metal creature went kitchenward for more dishes. "I've never been served better."

"Thank your grandfather," replied Buckalew, who was not eating, perhaps having had a meal earlier. "Dr. Stover made all these very successful machine-servitors now in use throughout Pulambar."

Stover had heard that. But his grandfather had ceased his robot building long ago. Why? Perhaps it was because his latest work, the problem of the Martian water shortage, had absorbed him.

"They aren't exactly alive, are they?" the young man asked Buckalew.

Buckalew's dark head shook, rather somberly. "No. They're only keyed to limited behavior-patterns. This one is good for personal service, others as mechanics' helpers, some of the best as calculators or clerks. But—" He broke off. "Where do you want to go first? I'm at your service, Dillon."

Stover wiped his mouth. "I suppose that business had better come before any pleasures. I'm here to look at drought conditions. Can you help me there?"

"Of course." Buckalew went to a wireless telephone instrument at the wall. "Short-shot rocket," he ordered into it, and led the way out upon the front balcony.

By bright daylight Stover now saw Pulambar spread far below the tower in which Buckalew lived.

Martians built Pulambar long ago at the apex of that forked expanse of verdure called Fastigium Aryn by Earth's old astronomers. Their world was dying in spite of science and toil, and in a pleasure city the doom might be forgotten. Pulambar had its foundations in the one lake left on Mars—canals for streets, open pools for squares, throngs of motorized gondolas and barges.

This was all the more wondrous since the rest of the planet fairly famished for water. Above towered clifflike buildings of every bright plastic material, rimmed with walks, strung with colored lights, balconied with gardens, spouting music and glare and gaiety, and crowded with tourists of all kinds and from all planets. If the laughter was a trifle hysterical, so much the better.

Above this massed roar and chatter rose towers and spires from the blocky masses of buildings. Here was Pulambar's upper segment—Tower Town, where wealth and society reigned. A world of its own, as Stover saw it, the highest peaks a good two miles from ground level and strung together with a silvery web of wire walkways and trolley tracks. Independent of the coarser turmoil below, it needed no such turmoil, having plenty of its own. It had its own law, sophistication; its own standard, glitter; its own ruler, bad but brilliant, Mace Malbrook.

Of all these things Stover had only dreamed in the simple and sober surroundings of his boyhood. Orphaned at six, he had gone to dwell with his grandfather, the doctor, at the laboratory farm in the Ozarks. Study, exercise, health—all those his grandfather had supervised, making him into a towering athlete and something of a journeyman scientist. But the old man had always discouraged long jaunts even to such places as St. Louis, the World Capitol, let alone to other planets. Well, thought Stover, he was able all the better to savor the excitement of the great Pleasure City of Mars.

"I'm certainly pro-Pulambar," he said to Buckalew, and he meant it.

"Here's our rocket cab," replied Buckalew, as a cartridge-shaped vehicle swam to the balcony railing. They entered the closed passenger compartment at the rear. "Tour us over the desert," Buckalew ordered the pilot through a speaking tube.

Away over the complex glitter of Pulambar they soared, turning their stern-blasts to the fork of scrubby vegetation that cuddled the lake-based city. Beyond and below Stover could see the desert, rusty red and blank.

"Looks as if it needs a drink bad," he said to Buckalew. "No wonder nobody lives in it."

"Oh, people live in it," surprisingly replied Buckalew. "Martians aren't as numerous as Terrestrials, but there's not enough good land for what there are." Again he addressed the speaking tube: "Pilot, go lower and slower."

The rocket dipped down. Stover could see the desert features more plainly, dunes, draws, expanses of red sand.

Buckalew pointed.

"You see that dark blotch like mold down there?" he asked. "It's a sign of life. Set us down by that hutch, pilot."

A minute later the cab dropped gently to the sand. Buckalew and Stover emerged.

Stover looked curiously at the blisterlike protuberance a few yards away. It rose perhaps five feet from the sand, and was twice that in diameter. At first sight it seemed of dull dark stuff, but then he saw that it was a semi-transparent shell, with clumpy vegetation inside.

"Come close," said Buckalew, and they walked up to the blister. "This is the desert camp of a Martian."

Inside the hummock grew a single bush or shrub. Its roots were deep in the sand, its broad-leafed branches spread out inside the shell to receive the sunlight.

Beneath those branches sprawled what looked some-thing like four big, limp spiders.

"Martians," said Buckalew.

Stover stared. The few Martians he had seen on Earth wore braces and garments to hold them erect in semi-Terrestrial posture. These, naked and unharnessed, showed as having soft bladder-bodies, each with six whip-like tentacles. Their heads, pink and covered with petal-like sense organs, all turned close to the big shrub. Stover saw that each of the Martians held a long pipe or tube in its tentacles, one end in the mouth orifice among the face petals. The other end of the pipe quested among the leaves of the shrub.

"They are probing for water to keep them alive," Buckalew explained.

Then Stover understood. The shrub's roots, deep and wide in the sand, drew to themselves all surrounding moisture. It concentrated in the leafage, a droplet at a time. These wretched creatures sealed the plant in lest the precious damp be lost by evaporation.

"Martians make such enclosures from the glassy sili-cates in the sand," Buckalew was saying. "A Martian doesn't need much food—a few ounces of concentrate will last for ever so long. What they need is a little wa-ter, and the plant can give that for a time."

"For a time?" repeated Stover, staring again. "What happens when the plant's water-production gives out?"

"The Martians die."

"That must happen pretty often," said Stover soberly, unconsciously quoting *Through the Looking-Glass.*

It may be that Buckalew was deliberate in rejoining, from the same work:

"It always happens."

He stepped close to the sealed shelter, tapping on it with his knuckles. A Martian wriggled toward them.

Buckalew held up something he had brought in the rocket—a clayware water jug, stoppered carefully, holding about two quarts. The Martian inside made frantic, appealing gestures.

Buckalew set the jug close to the foot of the glass wall, and the Martian burrowed quickly under, snatching it.

Stover turned away, almost shuddering, from the sight of all the creatures crowding around that pitiful container of water.

"We go back now," said Buckalew, and they re-entered the cab.

Stover was somewhat pale under his healthy skin.

"This is ghastly," he said at last. "They have to suck up to that poor plant—ugh!"

"That is but one little encampment of many such," Buckalew told him. "Shall we stop at the fringe of Pulambar when we go back? To see the water-lines?"

"Water-lines?" repeated Stover. "Are they like bread-lines used to be on Earth?"

"Very much like that. Long processions of wretched poor, coming to get half-pint rations."

"I don't want to see that," Stover told him. "Let's get back to something gay."

"Back to my apartment," Buckalew told the pilot. To Stover he said: "We'll visit the Zaarr tonight—best public house in Pulambar."

CHAPTER II

Martian Holiday

ZAARR, in the slurring language of Mars, means Unattached. The public house mentioned by Buckalew was almost what the name implied—a dome-shaped edifice of silvery alloy, floating at a fixed point among four tall towers. From each tower flashed a gravity-lock beam, like an invisible girder, to moor the Zaarr in space. The only way there was by heliocopter, short-shot rocket, or other sky vehicle.

Admission was by appointment, costing high.

The table of Stover and Buckalew was at the raised end of the inner hall. Below them, the crystal floor revealed the pageant of Pulambar's lower levels a mile below. A Terrestrial orchestra, best in the Solar System, played in a central pit while brigades of entertainers performed. Over all, at the highest point of the dome, hung a light that changed tint constantly, a Martian "joy-lamp" whose rays brought elevated visions to Martians, and sometimes madness and violence to Terrestrials.

It would have been more of a treat to Stover if he hadn't kept remembering that other dome-shaped structure he had seen earlier where four wretched Martian paupers prisoned themselves to suck miserable life from the distillations of a poor plant. Again he wanted to shudder, and beat down the impulse. He was here to enjoy himself. Pulambar was the most exciting spot in the habitable universe, and the Zaarr it's greatest focus of fun.

He contrasted all this with his familiar Ozark home, white utilitarian walls, laboratory benches and surrounding greenery, inhabited by sober technicians and caretakers. In the changing joy-light, the guests seemed the more exotic and picturesque, clad in all colors and richnesses, their hair—male and female—dressed and curled and often dyed with gay colors.

No hysterical howl at the Zaarr. Here was society, restrained even under the joy-lamp. Most of them were Terrestrials or Terrestrial-descended Jovians, for such had most of the money in the System. There was just a sprinkling of Venusians, and the only Martian anywhere in sight was the proprietor, Prrala, over by a service entrance.

The attendants were robots, great gleaming bodies with cunning joints and faces blank save for round white lamps.

To Dillon Stover, who had never seen such things, they looked like animated suits of ancient armor.

"Intriguing to notice," he said to Buckalew in his gentle voice, "how, after so many millennia, people still turn to the same basic items of entertainment—sweet sounds, stimulating drink or other narcotics, palatable food, and parades of lovely girls." He eyed with mild admiration the slim, tawny young woman who stood on the brink of the orchestra pit and sang a farce novelty number about a rich man who was sick.

"That entertainer," commented Buckalew, "might fit as well into an ancient Roman banquet scene, a tournament of song in old Thuringia, or the New York theatrical world of the twentieth century. There's been nothing new, my young friend, since the day before history's dawn."

Stover looked at the girl with more interest. He replied only because Buckalew seemed to expect some sort of a reply.

"That's new, to me at least," he argued, jerking his head toward the joylamp. It shot a sudden white beam to light him up, and he was revealed as easily the handsomest man of all those present.

Even sitting, he showed great length and volume of muscle inside his close-fitting cloth of gold. His hair, shorter than fashionable, gleamed only less golden than his tunic.

His young face was made strong by the bony aggressiveness of nose and jaw. His intensely blue eyes carried the darkly glowing light of hot temper in them.

"I'm trying not to let that lamp stir me up too much," he went on. "It seems to intoxicate everybody except you."

"I'm saturated," retorted Buckalew. "Well, how will you like to go to work when this holiday's done?"

"Let work be left out of the present conversation," Stover pleaded. "I want complete relaxation and excitement. Tomorrow I'll visit the lower levels, Mr. Buckalew."

"They get rough down there," Buckalew reminded. "Lots of rowdy customers—space-crews on leave, confidence men, and all that."

"I can get rough, too," said Stover. "You know, I feel a scrap coming on. I won't deny I'm a fighter by temperament, Mr. Buckalew."

"Your grandfather was a fighter, too," said Buckalew, his deep, dark eyes introspective as if gazing down corridors of the past. "Much like you in his youth—big, happy, strong. Later he turned his back on all this, Pulambar and other pleasure points, and became the highest rated natural philosopher of his time. You inherited his job, you tell me—the unfinished job of perfecting the condenser ray."

"A job that ought to be done," nodded Stover.

"A job that must be done," rejoined Buckalew earnestly. "You tell me how much you like Pulambar, but doesn't that extravagant lake down below make you feel a trifle vicious? Don't you stop to think that the poor thirsty deserts of Mars could suck up a thousand times that much water without showing it?

"Don't you understand how this great planet, with what was once the greatest civilization in the known universe, is dying for lack of water—or, rather, for the ability to keep that water? And that's what the condenser ray will do. By the way, you may call me Robert, if you like. That's what your grandfather called me."

Stover turned back to a remark he had begun earlier. "I said I'd like to fight—Robert. That's because I think, and keep thinking, of this man Malbrook who seems to own Pulambar and this wasteful lake and all. Why doesn't he divide the water with the unfortunate poor?"

"Because he's Malbrook," replied Buckalew shortly. "He won't like it, at that, if you make water too easy to get. That's what will happen if your condenser ray works. It'll condense all the water vapor that has been escaping up to now, giving rain and returning fertility to this planet."

"Grandfather used to talk like that," remembered Stover. "I'm not as brilliant as he is, but I'll work as hard—after awhile. Just now I want to get the ugly thought of those poor thirsty devils out of my mind. I'll have a drink."

"Your grandfather used to take *guil* in his wine," informed Buckalew.

Stover looked at his companion, and suddenly found it more believable that here was an old friend of his grandfather. For all the ungrayed hair and smooth face, Buckalew had eyes that might have been born with the first planets. Not old, but ageless. Stover began to frame in his mind a polite inquiry as to how these things might be. At that moment a strange voice, clear and low, broke in upon his meditations.

"Gentlemen, the management suggests that I say how glad we are to see you at the Zaarr once again."

Both rose, bowing. The speaker was the girl who had sung. "Please sit down," begged Stover, holding a chair.

She smiled and did so. Her eyes were large and dark, her chin smoothly pointed. Even without her heavy makeup she would be lovely. Beside Stover she seemed no larger than a child.

Buckalew signaled a robot waiter, who clanked across with drink, a healthful Terrestrial wine laced with powerful Jovian *guil.*

"This is a pleasure, Miss—" Stover stumbled.

"My name is Bee MacGowan," the singer supplied, smiling.

"I've been admiring your singing," added Stover, blushing. "A pleasure, I say."

"Not to that young man," murmured Buckalew, his eyes flicking toward a lean, glowering fellow who sat alone at a near table.

This guest, with his close-fitting black garments, the mantle flung over the back of his chair, and his pallid scowl beneath a profusion of wavy dark hair, might have sat for a burlesque portrait of Hamlet.

"Oh, he?" said Bee MacGowan. "He's a little difficult, but I owe him nothing. Anyway, this is only a professional conference, eh?"

Buckalew continued studying the youth with the angry face. "Isn't he Amyas Crofts, the son of a vice-president or something in Spaceways? Mmmm. You'd think a dark ray of the joy-lamp had flicked him, while a bright one strikes my young friend here. You're a bit of a joy-lamp yourself, Miss MacGowan."

It was Stover's turn to laugh. "Nothing affects Buckalew, though. Neither joy-lamp, nor wine. As a matter of fact, I've never seen him drink. His intoxication must be of the spirit."

Buckalew's smooth dark head bowed. "Yes, of the spirit. See, isn't that Mace Malbrook?"

The music had paused, and all stirred at their tables. One or two even rose, as though to greet high nobility. And as far as Pulambar's society was concerned high nobility was present.

Mace Malbrook was huge and soft, draped and folded around with a togalike mantle of fiery red. His huge arrogant head, crowned with luxuriant waves of chestnut hair, turned this way and that. His face was Romanly masterful, for all its softness. The eyes were bright and deep-set, like fires in caves. His mouth looked hard even as he smiled at the respectful hubbub around him.

"So that's the man who rules Pulambar," said young Dillon Stover.

"Just as his grandfather ruled when your grandfather and I were young together here," nodded Buckalew. "The Malbrooks and Fieldings have gathered most of the property rights and concessions in Pulambar. They're also partners in the Polar Corporation that distributes water by canal over Mars."

Malbrook was being offered the best table. But he had sighted the little group across the room.

"I don't like people who stare at me," said Stover audibly.

And those seated nearest him flinched as at a blasphemy. But he meant it. The great Malbrook was to him a rude water-thief, no more and no less.

"Easy, Dillon," counselled Buckalew softly. "Malbrook's the law here."

"What's the matter, Miss MacGowan," Stover asked the girl beside him. "You're pale. Does he frighten you?"

"I think he does," she replied softly and woefully.

Malbrook was striding across toward them. Reaching their table, he bowed with a heavy flourish. The room was expectantly silent.

"Aren't you the girl who sings?" he purred, as if sure of his welcome. "I have decided to give you some of my time and attention. These gentlemen will excuse you, I am sure." And he looked a command at Stover.

Dillon Stover stood up, towering over Malbrook, who was not particularly small.

"What do you mean by strutting up like this?" he demanded. "Who are you?"

Buckalew, too, rose. "After all, Malbrook, this is a trifle irregular," he began mildly, when Malbrook snapped him off.

"You know me, Buckalew, and you'd better not prate about irregularities. I could embarrass you considerably, with two words. Or even one—a word that begins with R." The deep, bright eyes turned to Stover again, raking him insolently. "And since you don't know me, youngster, wait until I speak to you before you start dictating. All I want from you is the company of this lady."

He put his hand on Bee MacGowan's shoulder. She twitched away. And Stover promptly knocked Mace Malbrook down. Just like that.

Even as he uppercut Malbrook's fleshy curve of jaw, Stover knew what would follow. This was a man of importance and power. There was going to be trouble. While Malbrook bounced on the crystal floor, Stover kicked his chair away and set himself to meet a rush of attackers.

It did not come. Dead silent, the people at the tables stood up, as at a significant moment. That was all. Stover, who would have gladly fought a dozen Pulambar sparks, felt a trifle silly.

Then several figures quietly approached—Prrala, the Martian proprietor, and a pair of robot servants, silvery bright and taller than Stover. Behind them came a slight, sinewy fellow in green and silver who stooped to assist Malbrook. On his feet again, Malbrook faced Stover, hard-eyed. One well-kept hand rubbed his jaw.

"You struck me," Malbrook said incredulously.

Stover could have laughed. "Indeed I did, and I'll do it again if you don't mend your manners."

Bee MacGowan was leaving, at a gesture from Prrala. The angry-faced youngster, Amyas Crofts, was following her and talking rapidly. Meanwhile, Malbrook eyed Stover with insolent menace.

"Fine physical specimen," he sighed. "Worth working on. We'll go further into the matter, of course."

Stover understood. A duel. The System in general scorned duels. In some places they were forbidden, but they happened in Pulambar. Anything could happen in Pulambar. Occasional mannered killings added spice to society. Just now, he was being chosen for a victim.

"Whenever you like," he replied. "Mr. Buckalew will act for me."

Prrala touched one of his robots, and the thing moved nearer to Stover, as if to prevent him from doing something or other. Robots were apt to overawe newcomers in Pulambar with their size and metallic appearance of strength, but Stover, a scientist from boyhood, knew them for what they were—clumsy, dull makeshifts that could do only the simpler tasks of waiting on mankind.

"Keep that tin soldier back," Stover warned, "or I'll smack him over."

"I only wissh that therre be no morre violent quarrrelling," said Prrala in his purring voice.

"There'll be no more quarreling here," promised the sinewy man in green and silver, turning to Stover. "What's your name? Stover? Before you go asking for challenges, better realize that Mr. Malbrook is the most accomplished duellist in Pulambar. You haven't a chance against him."

CHAPTER III

Sudden Death

THIS speech carried to almost every ear in the hall. Stover bowed.

"I can't withdraw, after that, without looking afraid. I'll fight your friend Malbrook very cheerfully, Mr.— Mr.—"

"Brome Fielding," supplied Buckalew in a worried voice, and Stover remembered that this was the name of Malbrook's partner in society and finance. "I wish, Dillon, that in some way—"

"Never mind, Buckalew," snarled Malbrook suddenly. "Don't try to talk him out of it. I've challenged, and he's accepted. Do I have to remind you again that you'd better do as I say?"

"That's enough," growled Stover so savagely that everybody faced him. "If it's killing Malbrook needs, I'll cooperate." His anger had risen steadily higher, but he felt cold and steady. "I begin to think he should have been killed long ago. Listen, everyone!" he shouted to the roomful. "Haven't many of you wanted to kill this strutting swine? Well, I'll do it for all of us."

Prrala, all flower-head and waving arm-tentacles, made little hisses and gestures of pacification. Buckalew swiftly caught Stover's arm, leading him into the vestibule. A helio-taxi hung there, and they got in and headed for their tower lodgings, Stover still protesting. The sky was doubly starry overhead, and the two moons of Mars, larger than Luna seems from Earth, gave them white light. Below beat up the welter of light and sound from the lower levels.

"It isn't as if you loved that girl, or even knew her well," reproved Buckalew. "If you did, it might be worth your while to commit suicide like this."

Stover cooled a bit. "How did I get into this position of kill or be killed?" he demanded. "I was minding my business. Up bobbed Malbrook to act a first-class pig. No man would endure—"

"Folk in Pulambar endure a lot from Malbrook," said Buckalew significantly.

And Stover remembered how Malbrook had snubbed Buckalew by a threat of exposure—exposure in one word, beginning with R. What could it be? Was Buckalew secretly plotting rebellion? But his own problem had better occupy his attention.

"Don't be so sure he can kill me, Robert," he growled, leaning back against the cushions of the flyer cabin. "What will this duel be with? Electro-automatics, ray sabers, MS-projectors, or just plain fists? I'm handy with all of them."

"Palambar duels aren't that simple. Malbrook, the party attacked, can choose his own weapons and conditions. He might make it under water, if he thought he swam better than you. Or with knives or acid hypodermics. It might be a cut of the cards, loser to drink poison—with cards stacked. Or in a dark room, each with a single-shot pistol, Malbrook choosing a room he knows well and which you've never entered. He's boss, I say. He can run this affair, like any affair in Pulambar, to suit himself."

"Thanks for the tip," said Stover, his lips hardening. "I'm to be slaughtered, then? But I'll make my own terms. Both of us to go armed, and start shooting or stabbing or raying on sight. That would make it fair, and Malbrook doesn't deserve even that."

"Well," said Buckalew, gazing from a port, "we're at our diggings. Judging from the flyers moored outside and the lights inside, we have company."

They had. Stepping from the hovering flyer to their balcony and handing their cloaks to the robot attendant, they entered to find a group of people, brilliantly dressed and set-faced, in their sitting-room.

First of these, Dillon Stover recognized tawny Bee MacGowan. For a moment it seemed as if she were alone before him, and most important—the trouble over her made her a responsibility and a comrade. Buckalew began making introductions.

"This, Dillon, is Miss Reynardine Phogor. And this is her guardian, Phogor of Venus. You've seen Mr. Amyas Crofts, but you haven't met him. You know Prrala, proprietor of the Zaarr; and Mr. Fielding, Mr. Malbrook's business associate."

"Also his second," added in Fielding. "I'm here to arrange matters. Malbrook, having choice of conditions, wants—"

"I don't care what he wants," interrupted Stover curtly. "I've just heard how duels are planned—framed, rather—in Pulambar. Nothing doing. Let us arm ourselves and fight on sight."

"Eh?" gasped Fielding. "That's not at all what Malbrook wants."

"I can well believe it," nodded Stover bleakly. "He's had things too much his own way here in Pulambar. He thinks he can insult ladies like Miss MacGowan and kill men like me, because he has the difference on his side. Well, I'm holding out for an even break."

All stared at Stover. Reynardine Phogor spoke first.

"I'm on the fringe of all this. I'd like information and explanation, Mr. Stover."

"If I can give you either." And Stover bowed courteously.

The girl was almost as tall for a woman as he for a man, of generous but graceful contour, with sultry dark beauty. Her hair, by careful processing, was fashionably "brindled"—broad streaks of pallor among the natural dark. Her tight gown gleamed with jewels. For a moment little Bee MacGowan seemed almost dull by comparison.

"Frankly, I thought I was on the best terms with Mace Malbrook," she was continuing. "We talked of marriage. Then he quarrels with you over this— this—" She gestured at Bee MacGowan.

The singer was pale but angry. "All I came here for was to see if I couldn't stop the duel some way," she protested.

Amyas Crofts snarled in his throat. "Speaking of marriage," he said, "consider any idea of that off between us, Bee."

"I never accepted you," Bee flung back.

There was a moment almost of concerted recriminations—Crofts, Reynardine Phogor and Bee MacGowan all at once execrating Malbrook. Bee MacGowan quieted first, as if ashamed of her exhibition. Then Fielding waved Crofts silent.

"When I tell Mr. Malbrook what you've said," he announced grimly, "he'll give you a challenge to follow this affair with Mr. Stover."

Crofts turned pale as ashes, but clenched his bony fists. Meanwhile Phogor, a richly clad Venusian with the wide mouth, pop eyes and mottled skin of a monstrous frog, was addressing his stepdaughter.

"Control yourself, Reynardine. I do not like this loud—"

"I don't like it, either!" she cried. "Daddy Phogor, it's no more fun for me than for you. But if I didn't fight for my man—" She whirled upon Bee MacGowan. "Survival of the fittest, you warbling little sneak—and I feel mighty fit. Well Mr. Stover? You promised to explain?"

"If you give me a chance," replied Stover quietly. "I had just met Miss MacGowan. We weren't beyond the first introductions when this Malbrook fellow swaggered up and made himself obnoxious. I hit him, and he challenged me. Just like that. And I demand a fifty-fifty chance. I think that covers everything."

Phogor boomed forth, loudly even for a Venusian.

"I did not know how things stood with my ward. If Malbrook offered marriage, then followed with this disgraceful conduct—" He broke off for a moment. Then, "Don't try to frighten me by staring, Fielding. You and Malbrook are absolute rulers here, but I'm important on Venus. I have money and power. I'll take care of myself and Reynardine."

"What brings you, Prrala?" Buckalew asked worriedly at this juncture.

The long-robed Martian bowed. "I wissh peace," he slurred out. "It will haarm my business if it iss rreporrted that a morrtal duel had itss sstarrt in my esstablisshment. I hope to brring about a bloodlesss ssettlement."

Stover waved the appeal away. "Sorry. Mr. Fielding fixed it so that I couldn't withdraw by telling how dangerous his friend is."

The Martian bowed. "Then I musst trry Mr. Malbrrook." He said farewells all around and departed.

"Malbrook won't listen, either," Fielding said as the door closed behind Prrala. "And when he hears those charges of foul play he won't like them. Nor, Buckalew, will he appreciate your standing behind Stover in that attitude."

Buckalew's eyes glittered. "Do you think I'll endure being bulldozed forever?" he demanded.

"You'd better endure it forever," warned Fielding.

"Someone should silence Malbrook's dirty mouth," said Buckalew hotly, and walked away across the floor.

Phogor moved doorward.

"Come, Reynardine," he said gravely. "You see the low valuation Mr. Malbrook places upon you and your feelings. Mr. Stover, I am inclined to wish you good luck."

Fielding laughed aloud. "You're optimistic. Malbrook will slay this insolent young spark with no effort. You, Phogor, will wish you hadn't spoken like that— and the rest of you, too." He took a step toward Bee MacGowan. "As for you, you little troublemaker—"

"Fielding, shall I give you the twin to that punch Malbrook got?" asked Stover harshly. "No? Then clear out."

In a few moments all the callers were gone but Bee MacGowan and young Crofts.

"Amyas," said the girl, "will you go on ahead? I have something I must ask Mr. Stover." When the youth had ungraciously departed she faced Stover. "I've done this to you," she accused herself tremulously. "Do you think that I might go to Malbrook and straighten this out?"

"Miss MacGowan," said Stover, "you seem to think that I stand greatly in fear of what that lardy bully can do. Give yourself no concern. The one to suffer will be Malbrook. There are graver reasons than a mere brawl."

"Drop it, Dillon!" pleaded Buckalew, returning from an inner room. "Malbrook and Fielding can do as they please. You don't stand a chance. Since you've refused a formal duel and threatened Malbrook, there'll be an

armed watch set. You may even be arrested. At the first
overt move you make—" Buckalew's long, fine fingers
snapped—"you'll be eliminated."

"They can't!" protested Stover.

"They can do anything—kill you and ruin me, just
like winking."

"I'll go to Malbrook," said Bee MacGowan again,
firmly.

"Come back!" cried Stover, hurrying after her. But
she was already gone. He reached the balcony just in
time to see her board a helio-car and soar away.

Stover pressed a button, setting aglow the signal for
an air-taxi to come. Then he returned to the sitting-
room.

"She'll only give Malbrook another chance to insult
her," he began, then saw that Buckalew had left the
room. He went to a locker and took from it an electro-
automatic pistol. Thrusting this into his girdle, he went
back to the balcony.

Well, the arbiter of Pulambar society was set on getting his blood, thought Stover. Mace Malbrook, starver
of the poor, killer of the thirsty, bully and snob and ty-
rant, might think the quarrel had started from a trifle,
but Stover's unpleasant experience of the afternoon,
coupled with the insult to Bee MacGowan and perhaps
stirred up by drink and joy-lamp, had helped launch that
blow in Malbrook's face. Now since death threatened
him, it was imperative that he strike first.

A flying car swooped close, and Stover sprang
aboard. "You know where Mace Malbrook lives?" he
asked the pilot.

"Who doesn't? Are you a friend of his, sir?"

"I'm an enemy of his—the man who's going to kill
him," replied Stover. "Take me to his place at once."

"Sure thing," chuckled the pilot, plainly wondering what sort of joke this glittering customer was pleased to make.

Malbrook lived in a broad central tower of Pulambar, one of the four or five tallest, proudly aloof from the others. Stover disembarked on a terraced balcony.

A jointed robot servitor tried to halt him, but a shove of his big hand swept the stupid thing clanking clumsily aside. He burst into a reception hall, richly and garishly furnished. Before an inner door sprawled something, another robot, its silvery body clad in the white coat of a valet. It was quite still and limp, the front of its glass face-lamp broken. Somebody else had been here, and in a nasty mood.

Stover stepped across the metal carcass, up a hall and into a lighted room beyond. He came face to face with Brome Fielding, who lounged on a settle outside a heavy metal panel-way.

"Where's Malbrook?" demanded Stover.

Fielding jerked his head at the panel. "Inside his private rooms. I think Prrala's with him, trying to talk him out of the duel. No use your trying the same thing; it's beyond apologies now." Fielding's eyes shifted to the pistol-butt at Stover's waist. "Why are you carrying that gun?"

"It's for Malbrook," said Stover. "Who smashed the robot outside?"

"You mean Malbrook's valet? I posted him there to keep people out. Phogor tried to get in with that step-daughter, and one or two others."

"The valet's wrecked," informed Stover. "Get out of my way. I'm going in after Malbrook."

Fielding made a snatch at Stover's gun, and the young Earthman dispassionately hooked a fist to his jaw. The fellow spun around and crumpled in a corner. Stover knocked on the panel ringingly.

"Open up, Malbrook," he called. "Either let me in, or come out. It's Stover. If we're going to fight, let's do it now."

Silence, for perhaps five seconds. Then:

A thunderous crash of sound and force rocked the apartment around like a skiff on a hurricane sea. Stover was hurled backward, the metal door upon him. He fell, wriggled out from under the slap, and came groggily to his feet. Where the door had been set was now an oblong of murky light. He faced it, pistol in hand. Whatever had happened wasn't enough to kill him. Let Malbrook show his head.

"Clumsy work!" he cried in challenge. "I'm still all in one piece. Show yourself, and we'll finish this business."

Fielding was getting up, shaky and half-stunned. "What—what—" he mumbled.

"Explosion," said Stover. "Inside. Your friend Malbrook tried some cheap trick, but it didn't work."

Fielding darted through the doorway. Inside, he screamed once, loudly and tremulously. A moment later he sprang back into view.

"Malbrook!" he cried. "He's—dead!"

CHAPTER IV

The Law in Pulambar

THAT news cleared Stover's buzzing head like a whiff of ammonia. He bounded past Fielding into Malbrook's private apartment.

The room was full of hot, choking vapor, the sybaritic luxury thrown into turmoil by the explosion. Platinum-and-velvet furniture was overturned, gorgeous hangings ripped to shreds, delicately tinted walls racked and bulged. Another step, and he almost stumbled over something. Mace Malbrook, judging by the rags of that fire-colored mantle. No person could be so shattered and live. Beside him lay another still form, a flower-headed Martian, still moving slightly.

Stooping, Stover picked up Prrala's bladdery body and bore it out into the hall. Fielding was quavering into a vision-phone.

"Send police! We have the corpse, yes—and the killer!" Spinning, he leveled a ray-thrower.

"You're under arrest, Stover," he said.

"Don't be a fool," snapped the other, laying Prrala upon the settle where Fielding had first been sitting.

The Martian finally appeared to regain consciousness.

"Sstoverr?" he slurred feebly. "Why did you do it?"

"I did nothing," Stover assured him. "Just as I knocked—"

Police were rushing in, big, hard-bodied men in silk-metal tunics of black. Most of them were of the Lower

Pulambar Patrol, but the leader wore the insignia of the Martio-Terrestrial League Service. He was gaunt and gray-templed, and his narrow eyes took in at a glance the still figure on the couch, Fielding with his leveled weapon, and the baffled, angry Stover.

"I'm Chief Agent Congreve," he introduced himself crisply. "What's what?"

Fielding gestured with the ray thrower. "Stover did it. He charged in, slapped me down, and—"

"I wasn't even inside," exploded Stover. "An explosion killed Malbrook and hurt Prrala here, almost getting me, too."

Congreve faced Fielding. "You saw this man do the killing?"

"No, he knocked me down, I tell you. But he and Malbrook had quarreled. He came here for a showdown."

Congreve turned to Stover. "How much of that's true?"

"All of it, except that someone beat me to it. I didn't kill Malbrook."

Two officers were inspecting the wrecked room. "Almost blown to pieces," reported one. "Can't be sure of the explosive."

"Then make sure," snapped Congreve. "Chemical tests, and hurry before the air freshens. Doctor, how's that hurt Martian?"

A Venusian, bending over Prrala, replied gravely.

"He is reviving a trifle. May speak—perhaps for the last time."

"Take a record," Congreve directed still another man, who produced a dictagraph from his belt-pouch. Then, to Stover: "If you killed Malbrook, why not save us both trouble and say so?"

"I didn't," repeated Stover. "That's enough for you."

"You're talking to the law," warned Congreve.

"I seem to be talking to a fool. Fielding's the only witness, and he admits he was unconscious when the blast went off."

"You came here to kill Malbrook," accused Fielding.

"That has nothing to do with it, I was too late to kill him."

The Venusian doctor spoke again. "Quiet. This patient is trying to speak." He needled stimulant into Prrala's neck. "Do your best," he urged the Martian. "Tell what happened."

One of Prrala's tentacles fluttered up toward Stover. "Thiss man killed Malbrook. I wass prressent."

"Prrala was trying to make peace," volunteered Fielding. "He was in Malbrook's room when—"

"Let him tell it," bade Congreve.

Prrala managed more words. "We thought we werre alone. But, while we sspoke, ssomeone appeared in the rroom with uss. Malbrrook sspoke: 'Sstoverr!' And I ssaw that it wass he."

"Prrala!" protested Stover. "I was outside."

"But I rrecognized you . . ." Prrala was growing weaker. "Grreat height—blond hairr—gold garrmentss—it wass you, Sstoverr. Why . . ."

"He's close to the brink," said Congreve. "Needle him again, Doctor. Prrala, tell us the rest."

"Little to tell . . . Malbrrook ssaid, 'Sstand back, orr I firre.' Sstover sseemed about to leap. Malbrrook firred an electrro-automatic . . . explosion . . . I know nothing morre.

His voice died away Stover knelt beside him.

"You say I'm the killer, Prrala. But did nobody come in while you were with Malbrook?"

He thought of his own visitors earlier in the evening. Each had wanted to see Malbrook. Prrala summoned his last strength.

"Yess . . . one came . . . interrupted uss forr a moment . . ."

"Who, Prrala? Who?"

"It wass . . ." The Martian fell limp and silent.

"Wake him, Doctor," urged Congreve. "He can't die now."

The chief agent was wrong. Prrala was already dead.

Silence. Then two more figures entered. A policeman reported.

"Look what I found prowling around, Chief. Pretty, eh?"

He held Bee MacGowan by one round, bare arm. She was drawn of face, but her eyes were steady and unafraid. Congreve beckoned her.

"You knew Malbrook, young woman?"

She nodded. "I wanted to ask a favor. His robot valet wouldn't let me in."

"Are you the one who wrecked that robot?" asked Congreve.

Bee MacGowan said nothing. Stover spoke for her.

"When was wrecking a robot such a crime? They're simple, cheap—fifty value-units is plenty to pay for the best of them. And Pulambar crawls with them."

"Take the young woman's name," ordered Congreve. Then, to Stover: "You talk too much. You're under arrest. Come to my office."

He slid a hand under Stover's elbow.

Torn between rage and bewilderment, Stover went with his captors to the police flyer. They sped across the starry night to an opening lower down in another tower and transferred to an elevator. Again descending, they came to an office. Congreve took the single chair, leaving Stover on his feet. Another officer held a dictograph.

"I give you one more chance to talk," said Congreve sternly.

"I tell you once more that I'm innocent!" yelled Stover, the hot temper that had brought him to this plight reasserting itself. "I had had a quarrel with Malbrook. I went there to fight him. But he died at the hand of some other man, and a good thing."

Congreve studied his prisoner. "Gold cloth. Big, swell-looking fellow. Rich. Popular. You'll be missed up in that high-tower set. They've got away with many a rough and silly thing, those idle-richers, but the murder of an important man like Malbrook is where simple law officers like me step in. You'll be made an example."

"While you take out your spite against the rich crowd by insulting me," said Stover acidly. "The real killer's getting far away."

"Hard to crack, this Stover," said Congreve to the man with the dictagraph. "Lock him up and let him think it over."

Again Stover was marched away, down a long corridor of gray metal to a row of doors at the end. One of these doors swung open. Stover stepped in.

The cell was metal-lined, about five feet broad by seven long, and barely high enough to clear Stover's blond curls. It had no window, only a ventilator, and the dimmest of blue lights. The sole furniture was a metal cot against the rear wall.

Congreve had followed Stover. "I'll put my cards on the table," he said, "because they're good enough cards to show. I know these things:

"You and Malbrook quarreled and were going to shoot it out. You came to his place, on your own confession, to have a showdown. He was shut in a special apartment built to defend him from any attack. The only way in was via the door, if it could be forced.

"A witness died saying that you were the guilty one. Nobody lies on his deathbed, Stover. Then there's Fielding's story, the report of a robot you pushed away to get in, and an air-taximan who says you told him you were going to kill Malbrook.

"Our tests show that the weapon was simple old-fashioned nitroglycerin. You're down on Martian registers as a research scientist from Earth. You could have brought or made such stuff easily. You've been ugly and threatening to numerous persons and defiant to me. All you can say now is, 'I didn't do it.' "

"And I didn't," flung out Stover once more.

"I think you did. I think you smashed that guard-robot at the front door, knocked down Fielding, and jimmied Malbrook's door some way. He shot at you, but that wouldn't make your plea of self-defense any good. You were invading his premises. You blew him up. Only the last words of Prrala kept you from covering yourself somehow. That's what I'm going to prove against you in a court of law. You'll pay for the crime with your own life. Good-night, Stover."

The door clanked shut. Stover, alone in his blue-dim cell, sat on the edge of the cot.

"They can't do this to me," he said aloud. "I'm innocent. Innocent men aren't found guilty—or are they? In Pulambar anything can happen."

Suddenly the light turned green, then yellow, then orange, then red.

Stover gazed up at it.

"Joy-lamp!" he muttered. "Not that I'm very joyous, though. What's the idea?"

The answer came to him. For ages, Martians had used these ever-changing rays as a pleasant stimulant. People of Earth, not conditioned as a race to such things, were frequently intoxicated, sometimes drugged—even driven mad—when they got too much joy-lamp. The police, apparently, had another use for the device. A man's wits, befuddled, would present less of an obstacle to questioning.

"Congreve will quiz me again," decided Stover. "Expect to find me off balance and unable to lie. What won't they think of next?"

But he had already told the truth, and it had not convinced. Checking back, he could see why not. He had quarreled with Malbrook, struck him, threatened to kill him on sight. He had gone forth to do it. He had been prevented, probably, because someone had done the same errand more promptly.

"Congreve won't swallow it," he told himself moodily. "I'll get thick-tongued and mouth all this out. He'll think it sounds even goopier than before, and give me the next jolt of the third degree, probably less pleasant than the joy-lamp."

He put his mind on the mystery again. Only proof, complete and convincing, would set him free. Someone else had killed Malbrook. Who?

His mind turned to the visitors who had discussed the proposed duel at his quarters. Each, as it happened, had sworn to visit Malbrook, for good or ill. Prrala had been the first to go, and was dead now. What of the others?

If he was to be fuddled by the joy-lamp, he had best make notes from which to argue. From his belt-pouch he took a small pad and a pencil. Waiting for the joy-lamp to give him a clear violet light, he began to write.

REYNARDINE PHOGOR

Character: Proud, hard, beautiful. Jealous of Malbrook's attentions to Bee MacGowan. Considers herself scorned. Probably capable of killing.

Possible Motive: Jealousy and injured pride.

Possible mode of murder: As Malbrook's fiancée, may have known how to enter his specially defended apartment.

PHOGOR

Character: Venusian. People of Venus consider murder lightly.

Possible motive: Knew nothing of stepdaughter's engagement to Malbrook until incident of challenge. Surprised, resentful.

Possible mode of murder: May have pushed in, as I am accused of doing. Got there ahead of Prrala and Fielding, hid in room before it was closed.

ROBERT BUCKALEW

Character: Mysterious, witty, likeable. Probably would kill if he decided it necessary.

Possible motive: Malbrook threatened him with exposure of some deadly secret.

Possible mode of murder: As close acquaintance of Malbrook, with quarrel and threat of long standing, may have previously planned way in and method of killing. If so, must have left for Malbrook's when I did.

AMYAS CROFTS

Character: Callow, vicious, vain, hotheaded.

Possible motive: In love with Bee MacGowan—jealous of Malbrook. Also, it was suggested that Malbrook might kill him in later duel.

Possible mode of murder: Stealthy or violent entry.

BROME FIELDING

Character: Ruthless, haughty, shrewd. Long associated with Malbrook.

Possible motive: Possible quarrel, personal or business. Both men masterful and violent, capable of such clash.

Possible mode of murder: Hard to figure out—accomplice or illusion.

MY OWN DEFENSE

Despite identification of myself as killer, there may have been impersonation—mask, wig, stilts for height, costume. Light not too good, appearance brief, Prrala's testimony given in great pain and at moment of death.

Explosion occurred in chamber while I was out. Recommend more thorough investigation.

This last seemed hard to write. Stover felt weary, half-blind. He put away his notes and tried to lie on the cot. Then he looked up at the joy-lamp, and smiled as if in inspiration. He slid under the bed.

Thus shaded from the befuddling glow, he felt his head wash clear again. Maybe he wouldn't be thinking at too great a disadvantage, after all.

CHAPTER V

The Escape

TIME PASSED. Stover slept, then awakened. His door was being opened. A man in uniform entered. Congreve? No, this was a sturdy, dark fellow with a tray of dishes, plainly a jailor of some sort. Two pale eyes, strange in that swarthy face, looked at Stover.

"What are you doing down there?" demanded the jailer. "Here, the chief thought you might like some rations."

Stover rose. He felt no more intoxication. "What time is it, approximately?" he asked.

"Evening. Past sundown. I'm going off duty in five minutes." The jailer set the tray on the bed.

Stover, then, had slept for hours, and it was dark once more. "Wait," he said. "I want to talk to you."

What he really wanted was a chance to study the jailer's face, for inspiration had come to him; but the chance was short.

"Against orders," he was told. "I've got to push along."

And the man left. But not before Stover had seen that he had a face somewhat like his own—big, straight nose, square jaw, bright blue eyes. The difference was in complexion—black hair and brown skin. And complexion could be changed.

First Stover inspected the contents of the tray. Most of the food was synthetic—meat paste, acid drink, a salad of cellophane-like sheets of roughage. What interested him most was a hunk of butter substitute. Sitting down beside the tray, Stover again produced the pencil from his belt-pouch.

With his strong fingers he split the wood and extracted the soft, crumbly lead. Breaking the black stick in two, he rubbed the two bits together over the butter. The sooty powder fell thickly, and Stover mixed it in with a fork, producing a wad of gleaming oily-black substance. Quickly he rubbed this into his blond hair, smoothing out its curls and plastering them to his skull. The tray, which was of shiny metal, served as a mirror. He looked about as dark-haired as the jailer.

"So far so good," he approved, and again overhauled the food-stuffs. The cup of acid drink seemed most promising. Once more he explored his pouch. It yielded two cigarettes. Splitting these, he dropped the shreds of tobacco into the cup. Judicious stirring and mixing provided him with a coffee-brown liquid. He made tests on the back of his hand, deepened the tint with the last of his powdered pencil-lead. Finally he doffed his stylish golden garments.

With palmful after palmful of the makeshift dye, he stained his big body and limbs, using the tray as a mirror while he darkened his face and neck as well. His hands and feet were also treated. Now he appeared as a naked, swarthy personage with strangely pale eyes who was not too different from the jailer.

He waited some time longer, to be sure that enough time had passed to insure the fellow being well off duty. Then he sprang to the door, beating on it with his fists.

"Help! Help!" he roared. "I'm penned up! Prisoner's escaping!"

Answering commotion sounded outside. Then a harsh voice:

"What's the racket in there, Stover?"

"Stover's gone," he made gruff reply. "When I brought him his food, he jumped on me, knocked me out and took my clothes. He got away!"

"Oh, it's Dellis?" The door was quickly unlocked and opened.

Remembering that the jailor he impersonated had not matched his inches, Stover crouched on the floor. The shifting light of the joy-lamp helped his disguise, and the police guard who looked in was deceived for the moment.

"What happened, did you say?"

"Can't you see?" Stover yelled in feigned impatience. "He knocked me out and took my uniform. There's his rig." He pointed with one stained hand at his own crumpled garments in a corner. "While you stand there, he's probably clear away."

"Well, come out of there," the guard told him. "Wrap a blanket from the cot around you. We've got to make a report, quick!"

Stover wrapped himself up as directed, taking care to slump and so approximate the lesser height of the jailor Dellis. Under the blanket he brought along his felt and pouch. But he did not intend to appear before Congreve or other too-observant officers. Reeling, he supported himself against the door-jamb.

"I still feel shaky."

"Here, then." Another guard had come up, and the first guard beckoned him. "Take Dellis to the locker room while I report to the front office. That big society lad, Stover, got away."

Leaning heavily on the newcomer's arm, and half-swaddling his stained head and body in the blanket, Stover allowed himself to be helped down another corridor and into a long room lined with lockers. Against one wall was a cot, where he dropped with a moan.

"Hurt bad, Dellis?" asked the guard who had brought him.

"I hope not," sighed Stover. "Let me lie here for a while."

The other left. As the door closed, Stover sprang up and to a lavatory. Scrubbing violently, he cleansed hair and body of his messy disguise. Then he opened locker after locker. Most of the clothes inside were too small, but he found a drab civilian tunic in one, breeches in another, and boots in a third, all of them fair fits. Thus properly clad, he donned his own pouch and girdle and went to a window.

The level of the cells was still high above the noise and glow of the canal levels. A man less desperate might feel giddy, but Stover had no time for phobias. He must be free to find and convict the true murderer of Malbrook. Only thus could he hope to survive.

Quickly he ripped the blanket into half a dozen strips. Knotting these into a rope, he tied one end to a bracket-like fixture on the outer sill. A moment later he was sliding down into the night.

The gravity of Mars being barely four-tenths that of Earth, Stover's huge body weighed no more than eighty pounds as it swung to the cord of knotted blankets. Even so, he needed all of his nerve, strength and agility for what he planned to do.

A few seconds brought him to the end of his line, thirty feet below the window-sill. There were no windows or other openings at that point, and no projections on the smooth concrete wall, only a metal tube, barely an inch in diameter, that housed some slender power lines and ran vertically beside him. Every fifty feet or so it was clamped to the wall by a big staple. One such staple held it at the point where Stover dangled.

He looked in the other direction. Ten or twelve yards opposite was another building, with many lighted windows. Given a solid footing, he might have tried to leap. As it was, he must bridge the gap otherwise. He hung to his blanket-cord with one hand while he tugged and tore at the metal tubing. It was none too tough, and broke just at the staple. A jerk parted the wires inside. He tested the broken tube. It was springy and gave some resistance, but would it be enough? He could only try, with a prayer to all the gods of all the planets.

Grasping the tube with both hands, he quitted his cord. There he hung for a moment, like a beetle on a grass-stalk. Then the tube began to buckle outward at the staple clamp some fifty feet below. Stover's eighty pounds of weight swung it out across the chasm. He dared not look at the depths below. His eyes, turned overhead, watched the crawl of Deimos' disk across the starry sky. The tube was bending swiftly now—he was traveling out and down in a swift arc.

Ping! The tube broke at the lower staple. At the same instant Stover felt his shoulder brush against the wall of the building opposite. He let go of the tube, tried to clutch a window sill, and missed. He felt suddenly sick as he slid down the crag of concrete. His boot-heels smacked on a sill below, flew from it, and he made another desperate grasp. This time he made good his hold, and swung there, staring in.

The sizeable room was garishly lighted. People stood or sat inside, close-packed around tables. There was music from a radio tuned in on Earth, and a cheerful hubbub of everyone talking and laughing. At the table nearest the window were men and women in middle-class celebration clothes.

One of them flourished his loose-clenched fist, then brought it down and whipped it open. Out danced two pale cubes with black spots on their faces.

Dice—a game known when the pyramids were new, perhaps in the pre-civilized days before. Dice, which in ancient Rome had gained and lost mighty fortunes; which had delighted such rulers as Henry VIII of England, and such philosophers as Samuel L. Clemens of America. Dice, the one gambling game which had lasted to the thirtieth century.

"Game-dive," panted Stover. "Crowded, confused, relaxed. No worry about murders. I'll go in."

He worked along the sill, toward the next window. It was too far for his arms to span, but he spun his body sidewise, hooked a boot-toe within, let go and hurled himself across the sill and in.

He was in a private dining-room. A man and a woman sat at a table strewn with dishes, smirking affectionately at each other. As Stover drew himself up, the woman gave a little smothered cry of alarm and shrank into her chair. The man rose.

"Listen," he snarled to her, "if you say this is your husband, I'll tell you I'm too old for such a blackmail game—"

"I'm nobody's husband," Stover interrupted. "I just climbed in on a bet. Thought it was a game-dive."

"You're one window mistaken," the man said. "Get out of here."

Stover apologized and walked through a door, into the crowd beyond.

At the large central table, "indemnity" was being played. This old space-pirate game was almost as simple as blackjack and simpler than roulette. Each player could call for a card at each deal, or could refuse. Only those whose cards were of the same color stayed in.

When all were satisfied, unretired players totaled the values of their cards, and high man won both stakes and deal. The money, which could be won or lost swiftly, was the chief excitement.

Stover carried a sheaf of value-notes in his pouch, most of them in thousand-unit denominations. Entering the game, he lost twice and then won a big pot and the deal. As he distributed the cards, the radio music ceased.

"Late news," said an announcer's voice, and the vision-screen across the room lighted up.

Upon it, huge and stern, appeared a man's head and uniformed shoulders. Congreve!

"We're cutting in to enlist the help of all law-abiding listeners," said Congreve's magnified voice, and all play ceased as attentions turned to him. "Yesterday a murder occurred in the upper tower section. Mace Malbrook—"

The rest was momentarily drowned by a chorus of cries. Everyone had heard of Malbrook. Then silence again.

"—but the murderer escaped," Congreve was informing whatever worlds might hear. "Every officer is searching for him, and a reward of twenty thousand value-units is being offered by Mr. Gillan Fielding, partner of the murdered man, for any information leading to the capture of—"

"Twenty thou!" ejaculated a man near Stover. "I'd like to pick that up. I'd open a dive like this myself."

"Not me," chimed in someone else. "I'd try to buy into the water monopoly run by the Malbrook-Fielding combine. That's where the dough is on Mars. Every year the rates get higher and the demand bigger. Twenty thousand units, invested now—"

"Listen to the description," growled a man tersely.

"—twenty-three years old, very large and strong," Congreve was saying. "Six-feet-three, Earth measurement. Terrestrial weight, about two hundred pounds. Martian weight, about eighty. Smooth-shaven, blond hair, strong features. Well educated, a scientist, pleasing personality. Escaped in clothes stolen from police."

"He sounds like a television hero," breathed a girl in the crowd.

"To supplement this description, I will exhibit a late photograph of Dillon Stover, accused of the murder of Mace Malbrook."

Congreve's hand rose into view, with a rectangular piece of board. The vision-screen concentrated upon it, making it larger and clearer until it filled the entire screen, showing a vivid color-photo, taken three days before. Stover showed erect, tall, smiling and carefree. He was wearing his golden costume, which seemed doubly bright on the screen. The girl who had spoken before now gave vent to a whistle as of admiration.

"What a prince!" she cried.

Congreve's face returned. "I thank you," he said. The screen darkened, and the music resumed.

CHAPTER VI

The Girl in the Game-Dive

AT ONCE a hubbub of chatter broke out. People of the middle-class section of Pulambar were far noisier and more easily entertained than the bored sophisticates of the High-tower Set. Stover steadied his hands, completing the deal.

"Play cards," he said.

The man beside him looked at him sharply. "You know, stranger, to judge from that description, you might be the guy they're after."

"I was thinking the same thing," nodded Stover. "I'm about that size and age, and blond. Maybe I ought to turn myself in for the reward. Who wants cards on second deal?"

"But the picture killed it," went on the man beside him. "That bird in gold wasn't anything like you."

"Personally, I thought he looked like a sissy," grunted Stover.

He lost the next hand, cashed in and casually left the table. The brief interlude of play had helped to calm and encourage him. He was free and lost from pursuit, with a plan of campaign beginning to form. He went toward the door.

"Wait, big man," said a clear voice behind him. It was the girl who had admired his photograph on the vision screen. She was compact but comely, with red-dyed hair and a flashing smile. "Where are you going?"

"Your way," replied Stover promptly, feeling that a girl on his arm would be additional disguise.

They went out together, approaching a series of doors that were marked ELEVATORS, but she drew him away.

"Come along," she said. "I know an express that will drop us straight to the canal level."

"Just what I want," said Stover quite truthfully, and let her lead him along a side-corridor. At the end was a metal door. "What's your name?" he asked her, to make conversation.

"Call me Gerda," she said. "Enter. And what shall I call you?"

"Parker," he improvised. They came into a small, messy-walled room with one barred window and a telephone in a niche. "Here, Gerda, where's the elevator? And don't dig your elbow into me like that."

She laughed. "There's no elevator, and this isn't my elbow. It's a gun."

He sprang away, and the weapon rose in her hand, a vicious electro-automatic. She handled it with a forbidding ease. Her other hand slipped shut the catch on the door.

"Don't try anything suicidal," she bade him. "You're my prisoner, Dillon Stover. That fake dumb stare won't help. I've seen several photos of you besides that one on the televiso, and I had you spotted as soon as you walked into the game-dive."

"You were sent after me?" demanded Stover, giving up the farce.

"A regiment of us were. We knew you hadn't gone far. It was my luck to run across you."

"Congratulations," said Stover. "But the police will be more flattering than I."

The girl who called herself Gerda shook her red-dyed head. "Congratulations are nice. But I know someone who will pay for you with something besides congratulations and twenty thousand value-units."

"Who?" snapped Stover, for he knew she meant the murderer.

"You'll see soon enough," she told him with one of her bright smiles, and put her free hand on the telephone.

"Wait," he begged. "You speak of cash. More than the twenty thousand value-units the police offer. How much more?"

"Oh," said Gerda, her eyes wise above the leveled gun. "At least half as much again."

"I'll double it," said Stover, and she drew her hand back from the telephone. "May I take the money from my belt-pouch?"

She nodded permission, and he produced his notes. With what he had won at indemnity, he had a little more than the forty thousand he had offered. Counting off the surplus, he folded it and began to return it to his pouch.

"Wait," said Gerda greedily. "I'll take the whole thing."

Stover reluctantly surrendered all his money. She took it, thrust it into her own pouch. Then without lowering her gun, she caught his outstretched left hand in hers. A quick movement and she had snapped something on his wrist.

"Bracelet," she said. "Police bracelet. Isn't it pretty?"

Stover lifted his arm, staring at the thing. It was a plain circlet of nickeled steel, with a hinge and a lock. It bore a spherical device with a dial. From that sphere came a soft whirring sound.

"What's it for?" demanded Stover, angrily.

Gerda chuckled above her gun. "Police bracelet," she said again. "It has a radio apparatus tuned to the waves of police headquarters. You don't feel anything now, but if you go, say, ten miles from here, your whole body will vibrate to the amplified waves, as though you were being subjected to a heavy rush of current. The farther you go, the more drastic and painful the effect. Fifty miles away, you'd be done for—your nervous system tortured to death."

She picked up the telephone and called a number.

"This is Gerda," she said into the transmitter. "You know—police undercover detail. I have somebody you're interested in."

"You're taking my money and now you're selling me to the police!" cried Stover in sudden comprehension.

Gerda merely smiled at him.

"Wait," she said into the instrument, and then to Stover: "Not to the police. To somebody who will pay more. I only put the bracelet on to prevent any accident. Try to get away from me, and you'll not get far. Now, stand easy—I haven't finished phoning."

She turned back to the instrument.

"You heard his voice," she cooed into the phone. "Is your price still offered? Then come at once to—"

Stover made a frenzied leap. An electro-automatic pellet zipped its way through his tousled hair even as he twisted the weapon away. Tucking Gerda's struggling body under one arm, he seized the telephone.

"This is Stover," he grated into it. "While this she-rat of yours bragged, I jumped her and took her gun away. I'll get you next. Who is this?"

A gasp over the wire. That was all.

"Then I'll come and get you without any help. You killed Malbrook, didn't you? You want to kill me before the law learns I'm innocent, don't you? But it won't

work! Don't count your Dillon Stovers before they're
dead and buried. Good-by until we meet for the showdown!"

He hung up, thrusting the captured gun into his tunic.
Despite Gerda's frantic resistance, he coolly repossessed
the money she had taken from him. Finally he bound her
hands with her own belt and gagged her with a strip torn
from her skirt. She glared above the gag.

"Good-by, my bewitching little doublecrosser," he
bade her. "Stick to stool-pigeoning. The police will back
you—if they don't catch you cheating. I'm going to
catch the blundering killer you tried to sell me to."

"You'll never get away," she raged, managing to spit
out through the gag. "That bracelet will bring you
crawling back here."

"I won't wear it long," he said grimly. "It looks
smashable."

"Try to cut or smash it," she dared. "There'll be an
explosion that will tear your arm off at the shoulder.
You'll not live through that. I'll be seeing you soon, big
man—seeing you on your knees!"

"Don't hold your breath until then," he answered
curtly.

Unfastening the door, he left, went down the hall and
came to a corridor which led to an exit. Moored there
was a speedy-looking rocket flyer. He sprang in, turned
on the power, and sailed up and away.

CHAPTER VII

Thirst

LIKE most young men of his day, Dillon Stover understood very well the workings of rocket craft. This pur-
loined one-seater was not the newest model, but it was
serviceable. He felt sudden elation. Nobody knew his
jumping-off place save the undercover girl, Gerda. By
the time she escaped even that faint trail would be lost.
She would think twice about warning the police. If she
appealed only to the unknown killer, and if that unknown killer came seeking him, Stover would like nothing better.

"First," he decided, "I must get to another town and
pose there under a new name and personality. I'll dope
out this thing, maybe make a deal with some law-
enforcement body that isn't too friendly with Congreve
and the Malbrook-Fielding combine—hello, this rocket
isn't any too well hung together at that. I feel a funny
vibration all up my left arm. Must come from the fuel-
feed lever."

He took his hand from the fuel-feed lever. The vibration still quivered his left arm, climbed and crawled into
his shoulder and chest.

"Whup!" said Stover aloud. "It's that bracelet!"

Gerda, whatever her shortcomings, had spoken the
plain truth regarding this bit of police equipment. At ten
miles, she had warned, his body would be shaken as by

a heavy rush of current. The vibration now possessed his whole body, and Stover felt sick.

The car swayed and bucked under his ill-steadied controls, and he righted it with an effort.

"This can't go on!" he muttered. "I'll set her down on the sand—I'm well outside the city—and see if I can't squirm out of that bracelet."

He nosed down, but his run of bad luck was well in. In descending, he went still farther from the police headquarters radio. In mid-flight, nausea possessed him. His sight went black, his brain whirled and drummed.

With one hand he strove to flatten out his flight for a landing, but the other—the hand that wore the bracelet—refused to do its work. There was a shock, a crash of sound, and Dillon Stover flew through the air like a football. He fell sprawling in dry, powdery sand.

On Earth, where his weight was more than double what it was on Mars, he probably would not have risen from such a heavy fall. As it was, he rose very shakily. The wrecked rocket was aflame. Overhead beamed the lights of other aircraft speeding to investigate.

"Got to get away from here," he told himself groggily. "Get away—"

He headed out into the desert. His feet sank into the dry sand as into fresh snow. The vibrations from the bracelet still tingled in his arm and chest, made his lungs pant and his heart race; but, on the ground and walking, they were more endurable. The fall had made his nose bleed, and somehow this relieved his distress for the time being. He walked on, on. His lesser Martian weight made travel swift for his Earth-trained muscles, for all the binding sand around his insteps and ankles.

Behind him the lights of rocket craft were settling around the fire. He hoped that their landings in the sand would obscure his footprints. Meanwhile, he wished that he had a drink, about a two-quart swig of water, such as Buckalew had given to the desert Martians.

Stover had not taken a drink since before his trip to Malbrook's. The liquid of his prison meal had been used to disguise him. And this arid place, far away from the city of Pulambar and its lake-evaporations, was drying, dehydrating, even in the chilly Martian night.

He made the best of two miles' journey away from the investigators, then stopped. Overhead hurtled the disc of Phobos, giving him light whereby to examine the bracelet that dealt him so much misery. It was not too tight upon his wrist. He poked a finger under it, twiddled it, then tugged.

A red-hot pain shot through his forearm, as though all his joints were being dislocated. He hastily took his finger away. Again he remembered the baleful words of Gerda: *It will tear your arm off at the shoulder.* Better let bad enough alone. Meanwhile, what wouldn't he give for a drink?

Trudging onward, he pondered, despite his efforts to turn his mind elsewhere, on drinkables. Cold lemonade on the kitchen table at his grandfather's home, a stein of beer at college, water trickling down a rock-face at Rogers, Arkansas, the multitudinous beverages at the Zaarr—even the acid drink he had used for his disguise at the prison. He tried to curse such thoughts away, but his voice was thick and his tongue swollen.

Stover was scientist enough to understand all this. The atmosphere of Mars was light, one-third that of Earth. Plenty of oxygen made it fairly breathable, but it was hungry for water. Mars had so little water to give, and that little did not stay long—the lesser gravity could not hold water vapor. And so, as the moisture in his body was sweated forth, it was fairly snatched from him. He was dehydrating, like a prune or a date in a Sahara breeze, like a clay brick in a kiln.

Thirst was making him forget the lesser agony of the bracelet.

"I'd give up anything for a drink," he thought. "A thousand dollars of my legacy. My house in the Ozarks, that once belonged to my grandfather. I'd give up—but hold on. As a criminal I have no property to give up. Who would help me, if anyone were here? Buckalew? I wonder. Phogor? I doubt it. Bee MacGowan? Poor thing, she'd probably do what she could for me. But how long can this go on?"

Not long. For soon Dillon Stover fell on his face.

He struggled up to his hands and knees. More than ever he was down to first principles, a four-legged creature again, as man had been ages ago, before civilization or even savagery, struggling for life against the bitterest of environment.

He didn't intend to be killed, unjustly or otherwise. It wasn't on the books. Not for Dillon Stover. He managed to get up again. His tongue was swollen between dry lips, his stout knees wavered under his weight that seemed even more than Earth weight. But he'd get away from pursuit. And he'd drink.

Water ahead!

Both moons were up now, and they showed him a gleaming, rippling pool. With trees on the far side. He gave a joyful croak, and tried to run toward it. Again he fell forward and crawled painfully to the brink.

There was no brink.

Mirage. Or imagination. Dillon Stover would have wept, but there were no tears in his evaporated eyes. He sat, elbows on knees, and struck his forehead with his knuckles.

A little recovery now, enough to know that the bracelet's vibration was increased to a sharp agony. He had come miles away from Pulambar. Suddenly he wished he were back, even in jail. After all, there was comfort there, a bed to lie in, and doctors—and water. The Martians were right to prize it. If he could only wet his lips and wash his eyes. Then he'd think a way out for himself.

The sun was going to come up.

That would be the end. The dry Martian night had almost done for him; the blazing sun would finish the job. Perhaps it was just as well to lie down and die as quickly as possible. In the back of his head a little cluster of scientific-thinking cells computed that his night in this desert approximated five days of such an experience on Earth. Few people could survive that, even if they were as strong as Dillon Stover, and got help at the eleventh hour. And here was no help.

Wasn't there? He saw a shiny, semi-transparent blister among the sands, catching the first rays of dawn.

Under that would be Martians, a water plant—and water. Ever so little of the precious stuff would be a blessing.

He crawled there somehow. Remembering how the Martians inside a similar structure had burrowed out to the jug Buckalew donated, Stover began to paw and dig with his hands. The sand came away in great scooped masses. He got his head and shoulders under the glass-like under-rim, poked like a mole into the interior.

Something crept toward him, a Martian dweller. It had one of the artificial larynxes, for it formed words he could understand:

"Who arre you? Why do you darre—"

"My name is Stover," he whispered a wretched reply. "Dillon Stover. I am dying without water. Help me. Just—"

And he fainted.

So this was heaven.

The old talk about harps and songs and jeweled furniture had been wrong. It was more like the Zaarr, that report. Heaven really consisted in lying still in delicious dampness, with a ten-times blessed trickle of liquid into your open mouth.

Stover's eyes, no longer dried out, opened. And he saw heaven as well as felt it. The dull-clouded inside of a semi-transparent dome, against which spread the long branches and broad leaves of a blue-gray bush was above him, while around him sprawled three bladder-bodied, six-tentacled, flower-faced Martians.

"Lie sstill," purred the one with an artificial voice-box. "You arre verry ssick—nearr to death."

"I'm not," protested Stover, and sat up.

His dusty garments, stolen in a police dressing-room, had been removed. His naked skin felt cool, moist, and relaxed. He touched his arm with a finger. There was a sleek damp to it, like the damp of a frog.

"Lie sstill," said the Martian spokesman again. "If you do not fearr ssickness, fearr then the coming of a ssearrch parrty."

Stover lay back at once in the neat sandy hollow where they had bedded him. "Are they looking for me?" he asked anxiously.

The flowery head of his informant nodded, Terrestrial fashion. "Thrree timess they have come herre to peerr in. We ssaw them coming, and each time we coverred you with ssand to hide you. We told them we knew nothing of a fugitive Terrresstrrial. A wind blew away yourr trrackss."

Stover was content to lie still now. "How long have I been here?" he asked.

"A day and a night. It iss now the ssecond forre-noon."

Back into Stover's wakening mind floated memory of all that had transpired to bring him here. So it was getting on toward noon. Three noons ago he had awakened in Buckalew's luxurious apartment, reckless and carefree. At noon the following day, he had been in the police cell, again sleeping. When the third noon came, he had lain senseless in this poor makeshift den where Martians huddled to keep life in themselves. And now—

"I'll be awake this noon," he said aloud. "I've got a lot of escaping to do." To the Martian he said: "Which way is the nearest city? Besides Pulambar, I mean."

A tentacle pointed away. "But you cannot travel by day, on foot and underr the ssun. Wait until night. We sshall help you then."

Once again Stover took a look about. He saw whence had come the trickle into his mouth. One of those drinking tubes had been thrust into the integument of a great branch above him. Since he was awake, the tip of the tube had been thriftily plugged. But he felt dry again, and as though reading that thought in his mind, the Martian who did the talking removed the plug.

"Drrink," he bade Stover, and Stover drank.

He pulled strongly on the tube, and a delicious spurt of plant-juice, free-flowing and pleasantly tart-sweet, filled his mouth. What joy to drink! What relief, what privilege.

He stopped sucking all at once.

"Plug that up," he commanded. "Isn't it very precious, that juice? How is there enough for me and for you others, too?"

Something like a deprecating chuckle came from his attendant. "Do not ssay the worrd 'enough', Dillon Sstover. On Marrss, therre iss no ssuch worrd ass 'enough'."

"You've been depriving yourselves to take care of me!" Stover marveled, almost accusingly. "Why? I'm a stranger, a vagabond, wanted by police, charged with murder."

CHAPTER VIII

The Hope of Mars

HE was suddenly aware that another dreadful pain was missing, the racking vibration of the bracelet. He lifted his left hand. The skin of it was scraped, broken in places, but the wrist was naked. The sinister metal ring was gone.

"How did you get it off of me?" he asked. "It was due to explode if you tinkered with it."

"And sso we did not tinkerr with it," was the calm reply. "Firrsst, a grreasse to make yourr hand and wrrisst verry sslipperry—then carreful prrying and tugging. We got the brracelet off without injurring it. We know how to deal with ssuch thingss. One of uss crrept forrth and laid the brracelet on the ssand farr frrom herre. It was picked up ass a clue by police ssearcherrs."

Dillon Stover sighed gratefully. Not only was he free of an awful agony, but there would now be no following of him by those who hunted him.

"I started to ask you," he resumed, "why you helped a stranger, a Terrestrial fugitive from the law, to so great an extent."

"You arre Dillon Sstoverr," said the Martian simply. "Beforre you lost yourr ssensssess, you told uss yourr name."

Stover looked his mystification. "But what difference—"

A tentacle pointed to a little niche across the dome-den. There nestled a shabby old radio, near which the other two Martians sprawled. The thing only whispered, but they were getting news of the universe.

"We have communicationss," the one with the voice-box told Stover. "We know what befell you in Pulam-barr, what charrge iss made by the officiates. But we know, alsso, why you came herre—to do the worrk begun by yourr grrandfatherr."

"The work of my grandfather," repeated Stover. He had almost forgotten it. "You mean the condenser-ray?"

"Yess. The hope of Marrss."

Stover had recovered enough to tell himself savagely that he had become short-sighted, selfish, craven. The Martian was right. He, Dillon Stover, meant the sole chance of a dying world for a new lease on life. He was fleeing for more than his own life.

"I know so little," he pleaded. "I've been here only three days, and for most of that time I've been running from both police and law-breakers. I have now a better idea of what water means to this planet, but—"

"Come, if you arre strrong enough," bade his helper.

Stover got up, having to stoop beneath the low dome, and made his way to the radio. Quickly the Martian turned on the television power, and a small screen lighted up. Tentacles turned dials.

Stover saw a gently rolling plain, grown over with hardy, tufty scrub, the chief vegetation of Mars. From it rose a vast and blocky structure, acres in extent. The construction seemed to be of massive concrete or plastic, reenforced by joinings and bands of metal. As the viewpoint of the television made the building grow larger and nearer by degrees, Stover saw that it had no visible doors or other apertures. Along walks at the top, and around railed ways at the bottom, walked armed

Martian guards in brace-harness to hold them upright. The roof bristled with ray-throwers and electro-automatic guns.

"A fort?" said Stover. "I thought Mars was at peace everywhere."

"Therre iss no peace in the conflict with drrought," his informant told him. "You ssee yonderr a rresservoirr. It holdss a gatherring of the mosst prreciouss thing on thiss planet—waterr."

"It has to be guarded like that?"

"Ssurrely. People would rrisk anything to ssteal a little—only a little. The only frree waterr on all thiss worrld iss in the guarrded and rresstricted city of Pulambar, frrom which you have fled."

The dial clicked, another scene showed itself. Stover saw a building with open front before which huddled and crept a line of wretched Martians. Each presented a document to an official. Each was grudgingly handed a small container, no larger than a cup. Stover turned his head away. With a sympathetic purr, his companion turned the radio off.

"Water-lines," muttered Stover. "Guarded reservoirs. Little camps like this—and nobody has enough water. Malbrook, who held the monopoly, did this to Mars."

"You sserrved uss well by killing him," said the Martian. "Come, I wissh to dampen yourr sskin again."

He would not take no for an answer. An application of the plant-juice refreshed Stover's thirsty body all over.

"Do not thank uss," deprecated the Martian. "We do thiss becausse, to rrepeat mysself, you arre the hope of Marrss. By deprriving ourrsselvess of waterr rrationss today, we arre prreparring you forr the tassk of winning uss plenty in the futurre."

"You're trying not to be noble," Stover smiled. "But what if I miss out? If I'm caught, or killed, or if I try to develop the ray and can't?"

"We sshall have played forr high sstakess, and losst."

Stover found his clothing, neatly folded away, and began to struggle into it.

"When nightfall comes, I go," he announced.

"The besst rrefuge among the nearr townss—" began his rescuer.

"I'm going back to Pulambar," said Stover grimly.

All three Martians turned toward him silently. They had no human eyes, yet he had the sense of being stared at.

"I mean it," he insisted. "Pulambar's the place. The lights will guide me, and this stuff on my skin will keep me from drying out too soon. I can get by the outer guards, because I'm Terrestrial with money in my pocket. I've got to find the real killer and first put myself in the clear."

"Then?" prompted the Martian with the voice-box.

"Then," and Stover's voice rang like a bell inside the little dome, "I'm going to perfect that condenser-ray. I was wrong to want to play around first. Buckalew was right to keep after me. You've shown me a duty I can't turn away from. That killer in Pulambar had better hold onto his hat, because I'm going to smack him right out from under it!"

Once more back on the bright streets of Pulambar, Stover skirted a building and came to a canal crossing full of music and carnival. Entrance to the city had been quite as easy as he had figured. No one had dreamed that the fugitive would circle back. He halted now to consider his next step.

A mortised gondola of the cabin type bore a yapping loud-speaker urging all to join a sight-seeing tour. Stover joined the welter of honeymooners, space-hands, clerks on holiday and similar rubberneckers. A crowd like that made good disguise, and the gondola would take him to a certain definite jumping-off place for his newly chosen goal.

He sat back in a shadowy corner of the vehicle. The guide lectured eloquently as he clamped shut the ports and took them on a brief dive to show the underwater foundations of Pulambar, fringed with the rare lakeweed that was to be seen nowhere else on Mars. Stover remembered yet again how Buckalew had exhorted him—it seemed centuries before—to work hard for the salvation of Mars by the condenser ray.

Peering from his port, he saw the enclosing water, only a saucerful compared to the oceans of Earth, but here a curiosity and a luxury. He remembered, too, how he had seen in the television a desert where dammed and covered reservoirs were guarded by armed Martian troops as the most precious treasure-vaults of the planet.

He brought back to mind the pitiful folk of other Martian communities, who must deny themselves everything to pay the rates for only a tiny supervised trickle of the fluid which was life to them. All this he could obviate if he finished the ray mechanism—if he ever had a chance to finish it.

"I may die from something worse than water shortage if I don't look sharp," he told himself.

In his role of tourist, he achieved an appearance of attention as a lens-window in the roof was set so that the gaping tourists might look their fill upon the magnified disk of crystal rock that was the hurtling moon Phobos. He did his best to seem casual as they approached the sixth or seventh public building for a supervised inspection.

"Architecture bureau," announced the guide, impressively as though it were something he himself had planned and created. "Pulambar belongs as you know, to one great group of interests. Every building, small and great, rich and simple, must be maintained by that company. Pulambar being Pulambar, everything must stay at its best and most beautiful. No repairs are skimped or delayed anywhere. Look about you!"

Leaving the gondola, they entered a lofty room fitted as a main office. Around the sides were desks at which workers, mostly Martians, toiled at reports or instruments. Tourist parties being frequent here, no attention was paid to the intruders. The guide marshaled his charges around an altar-like stand in the center of the floor, on which glowed something that at first glance seemed a luminous birthday cake with myriad candles. A second look revealed an exquisitely made miniature of a group of buildings. "A model of Pulambar," breathed someone, but the guide laughed in lofty negation.

"It's a three-dimensional reflection, an image. Here, focused by an intricate system of televiso rays, is an actual miniature image of the city. Observe the detail of buildings and towers. Look closely and you will see actual movement of gondolas on the little canals, and flying specks in the upper levels, denoting aircraft."

It was so. The sightseers stared raptly. Even Stover, his mind filled with other things, was impressed.

"If we could see microscopically," went on the guide, "we'd even make out ourselves standing inside this building. And yet this is only an image, a concentration of light rays." To demonstrate, he passed his hand through the gleaming structure. "This miniature keeps before the attention of the Bureau the city's state of affairs, showing if anything is wrong in building or service. For instance—"

His forefinger hovered above one of the tiny towers, a jewel-delicate upward thrust. Malbrook's tower!

"See that bright point of light? Something is wrong. And," the guide's voice shifted to a dramatic bass, "it happens to be something of grim tragedy. That, my friends, is the spot where the awful explosion-slaying of Mace Malbrook took place recently. The speck of brilliance shows that repairs are needed there. This is to be done right away—now that the police relinquish the place."

The tourists hung on his words. Stover glanced to a bulletin screen, where work-details were posted. It was as he hoped. Halfway down were three words:

MALBROOK TOWER—GIRRA

Malbrook's tower was to be serviced by a worker named Girra. The time was posted, too: tomorrow morning, very early. The rest of Stover's problem solved itself very easily.

The boredom of the desk-workers helped. None saw him slip away from the tourist throng at an opportune time, dart into a dark doorway and down into the lower regions of the repair department.

Here, along a bench, sat metallic, grotesque figures—robots off duty. Each bore on its chest-plate a switch by which the mechanical semblance of life could be turned off and conserved when the robot was not in use. Here, too, were benches with racks of tools, stacks of spare parts. Stover, who knew machinery well, went to work confidently. Selecting a wrench, he examined robot after robot, seeking the one which bore the name, in Martian and Terrestrial characters: Girra. He found it.

This was Girra's helper. As its master was off duty, so also was this robot. Quickly Stover unbolted its front, and from inside the torso unshipped great quantities of springs, wires, wheels and other works, rapidly distributing them in the proper heaps of spare parts. When he had completely emptied the shell, even to the big mittenlike hands, he got into it as though it were indeed the suit of ancient armor it so resembled.

He had trouble clasping the jointed arm and leg pieces and the helmetlike head upon himself, but he finally managed. Then he loosened the radium lamp from its frontal fastenings a bit, to give himself a little space through which to see. At last he sat on the bench to await the Martian who owned this robot.

CHAPTER IX

Scene of the Crime

THE police officer on duty in Mace Malbrook's reception hall made disgusted gestures to quiet all his interrogates.

"Now there's another of you pests at the door," he groaned. "Why can't regulations keep a murder spot from being all cluttered up with High-tower people who wangle special passes?"

He crossed to the door and opened it. "Thank heaven, this is somebody with legitimate business," he growled.

"Right," said the Martian outside. "I am Girra, from Arrchitecturre Burreau, come to ssurrvey damage and esstimate rrepairrs. Alsso my helperr."

"I was told to admit only one man," said the officer. "Your helper must go back."

Girra snorted in the midst of the petal-like foliage that covered his cranium. "My helperr iss a rrobot, not a man." His tentacle gestured to where, behind him, towered a tall, jointed figure of silvery-plated metal.

"All right," granted the officer, and stepped out of the way.

In waddled Girra, and behind him stumped the grotesquely human structure, its jointed arms loaded with instruments, tool-cases and notebooks. Robots were too common in Pulambar for this one to attract much attention.

When Girra and his companion had entered the wrecked chamber, Reynardine Phogor was first of the four visitors to speak again.

"Mace constantly mentioned a will," she told the officer. "It's here somewhere, and it leaves me a controlling interest in his affairs. As his intended wife, I have a right to search for it. That explosion couldn't have blown it out of existence. Perhaps—" And she glared across at Brome Fielding.

"If you suggest that I destroyed it for any purpose—" began Fielding.

"Oh, short it," pleaded the officer. "All requests or complaints must be made to Special Agent Congreve. I told you he'd be here any time."

"Then why doesn't he hurry?" rumbled Phogor from his seat beside his stepdaughter.

The fourth civilian visitor, Amyas Crofts, kept silent. He looked more haggard than ever, and more savage.

All these things Stover saw and heard through his robot disguise. He tried to assimilate every word, at the same time being helpful to Girra and maintaining his machine impersonation. It was a difficult task, but he succeeded.

His previous visit to Malbrook's apartment had been too full of stress and excitement. Only now was he able to observe and estimate.

The room, made cube-form of metal, was bulged in all directions as though it had tried to become spherical. Only the strength of its material and fastenings had kept it from ripping to shreds. As to that, only the solidity of the door-panel had saved Stover's own life. The furniture was badly wrecked, even its metal frames being twisted and splintered. Prrala, decided Stover, had been able to live for a few more moments only because Malbrook must have been standing between him and—and what?

The killer must have been tall, blond, and dressed in gold, to have been identified as himself. Stover scowled perplexedly inside the metal cranium of his disguise.

Girra was investigating a round hole, little more than thumb-size, on the forward wall. "Ssmall wrrench," he ordered, shooting out a tentacle.

Stover found the desired tool in a box and passed it over. With it Girra loosened the device, the mouth-rim of a ventilator tube. Inside was a tiny fan to blow enough air through so small an orifice. The tube itself was left whole behind the damaged wall, for it would not pull out.

"Rray," commanded Girra, and Stover found him a metal-solvent ray projector. Skillfully Girra cut away an area of the plating.

The ventilator was revealed, a down-curved tube, like the trap of a lavatory. At the lowest point was one of Malbrook's protective devices, a liquid solvent for any poisonous or smothering gas. Girra tested it by thrusting in a flexible probe, which came out wet.

"Ventilatorr iss in good orrderr," he announced.

As he turned away to other surveys, Stover dared move close to the opening and investigate for himself. The ventilator, he saw, fastened to another tube that led through the outer plating to Malbrook's hall.

"Why do you loiterr therre?" Girra was demanding. "Iss ssomething wrrong?"

Too late, Stover realized that robot helpers are supposed to be above curiosity or individuality of any kind. If Girra considered that something was faulty in his mechanism and started to remove a plate to rectify it— but the Martian, coming toward him, was suddenly attracted to the piece of plating he had cut away from the wall and which now swung loose by the rim-attachment of the ventilator tube.

"What iss thiss sstain?" he asked aloud. "It sseemss local. The patrrol chemisstss have overrlooked it. Chemical kit!"

Stover handed the kit over. Girra daubed on some liquids, stirred and fumbled, noted the reaction, and made another slurred pronouncement:

"A carrbohydrrate of peculiar prroporrtion. A ssynthetic that apprroximatess Terrresstrrial rrubberr. Melted elasscoid, perrhapss." He confronted Stover. "Now, then, rrepeat back to me thesse findingss."

Evidently the work-robot also served as a sort of stenographer, receiving spoken words and keeping them like notes on a dictograph. Stover had listened with both his hidden ears, and was able to comply.

"Ventilator in good order," he repeated. "Stain of carbohydrate resembling synthetic rubber, probably elascoid."

But he was unable to duplicate Girra's Martian accent with its doubled *s* and *r* sounds. Girra was half-intrigued, half-upset.

"Have thosse Burreau mechanicss fiddled with yourr sspeech-vibrratorr?" he demanded.

"They have fiddled," replied Stover on inspiration, thankful that his voice echoed inside the metal-headpiece like that of the average speaking robot.

"Then they sshall hearr frrom me," promised Girra balefully. "Only I sshall sserrvice my helperr herreafterr." He turned back to his work. "All innerr plating of thiss aparrtment to be rremoved and rreplaced. Lessserr injurriess may have affected adjoining aparrtmentss. Come."

They returned to the outer hall. Girra paused to examine the doorway from which the panel had been blown away.

"New jamb needed herre," he announced. "Had not that rroom been sso sstrongly made, thiss whole towerr might have been wrrecked."

Stover should have been paying attention like a good robot, but at that moment new figures entered. Congreve came first, grim and trim and masterful. Behind him came Buckalew, in brown velvet-faced tunic and half-boots, sober-faced and a trifle worried in manner. The four visitors all started toward Congreve at once.

"Mace Malbrook's will—" began Reynardine.

"My stepdaughter's interests—" boomed Phogor at the same time.

"Chief, these High-tower swells are driving me—" complained the officer on guard.

"If you haven't recaptured Stover by this time—" threatened Fielding.

All this made deafening confusion. Throwing up his hands, Congreve fairly roared a command for silence. It fell, and he spoke coldly.

"I told Stover himself, before he escaped, that you idle-richers had things too much your own way, and that I was going to show, in this case, that the law is some steps higher than money. If any of you think you're running this show for me you're wrong. I don't know what authorities got you passes to this place, but I declare them no good.

"Your interests all around will be looked after to the best ability of the police department, but none of you are more important than the capture and punishment of the murderer. Now get out, all of you except Buckalew."

"How does Buckalew enjoy a privilege that's denied us?" wrathfully bellowed Phogor.

"It's not a privilege," replied Congreve with a frosty smile. "If it will help clear this place, I will inform you that he's under suspicion as Stover's friend and host, and unable to explain his whereabouts on the night of the killing."

Amyas Crofts, who had not joined the confusion, now addressed Congreve. "Are you aware, sir, that Miss MacGowan has disappeared? I went to her lodgings an hour ago, and she was gone. Nobody knew when or how she had left, or where bound. With Stover at large, I'm afraid for her."

"Save your fears," called Bee MacGowan's clear voice as she entered.

All gazed as she walked up to Congreve.

"They said at your headquarters that you were here," she said. "I come to give myself up."

"Give yourself up!" echoed Buckalew, Congreve and Crofts together.

She smiled quietly, and nodded.

"I must make an admission," she went on, as if reciting. "I said once that I came here to interview Mr. Malbrook just at the time of his death. The capture of Mr. Stover took your minds off me without further questioning. Prrala, before his death, tried to say that someone had come into the apartment during his talk with Malbrook. I am that someone."

More silence. Congreve broke it.

"Do I understand," he said, "that you are confessing to the murder?"

"I neither confess nor deny," the girl answered, almost primly. "You are a criminologist. Find out for yourself."

"You're under arrest," Congreve told her.

CHAPTER X

The Second Explosion

GIRRA, finishing his work, returned to the outer balcony where his flying machine was moored. But he did not enter it at once. Instead, he selected a wrench from among his tools and turned upon the robot helper whose peculiar behavior he diagnosed as faulty mechanism.

"I darre not trrusst you in the flyerr while my attention iss occupied by operrating the mechanissm," he addressed the metal figure. "I had betterr examine yourr worrkss now, fix them if possible, or put you temporarrily out of commisssion if not."

He paused, out of patience. His servitor was actually retreating before him. "Sstand sstill!" commanded Girra, and pursued.

Stover backed up, thinking hard and desperately. Then he could back no farther. Girra had herded him into a corner, close against the railing. The Martian extended the wrench, fumbling at one of the bolts that held Stover's disguise-shell together.

A twist, a tug, and his secret would be out—Girra would perceive that inside the apparent robot was not a mass of mechanism but a living Terrestrial, very much wanted by police. And Stover did not care to be arrested just now. He had other plans.

Because he must, he put forth one hand in its metal sheathing and snatched the wrench from Girra's grasp. The Martian mechanic retreated in turn, dumbfounded beyond speech. Then, as Stover made a threatening flourish with the wrench, Girra dropped the kit of tools he carried and retreated toward the entrance to Malbrook's apartment.

"Help! Asssisstance!" he squalled. "My rrobot hass gone out of contrrol!"

He was gone, out of sight for a few moments. In that precious time Stover carried into action a quick plan of misdirection. From the fallen toolkit he snatched a thin, strong line, knotted one end to the railing and threw the other end free into the abyss below. Then he ducked back into a shallow corner as Girra rushed forth again, followed by the mystified and impatient policeman who had kept guard in the vestibule.

"Now then, now then," this policeman was grumbling, after the manner of policemen generally throughout all worlds and ages. "What happened, you say? Your robot—where is your robot?"

Girra ran to the railing. One tentacle caught the tethered end of the line.

"It hass climbed down thiss line!" he cried sagely. "Climbed down to lowerr levelss and escaped!"

"Never heard of a robot doing that," commented the policeman. He went to Girra's side, and also peered down. "Huh!" he grunted. "That's what comes of too much clockwork in those babies. They get into wild messes. We'd better call for Congreve."

They entered the vestibule again.

At once Stover ran to the moored flyer, got in and went soaring away.

Girra got back to the Bureau office in a hired vehicle. The mystery was deepened when there came a report from a far rooftop. An Architecture Bureau ship had landed there. Whoever had flown it was gone. Inside was a robot shell, with no machinery. Girra, smarting from reprimands by Congreve and his work superior, sought furiously for the culprit responsible for this state of affairs. He failed to find him because he did not know where and how to look.

The culprit in question had gone straight to the office of Special Agent Congreve. When that intelligent officer returned from the Malbrook tower Stover stood forth to give himself up.

"I'm doing this," said Stover, "because I want to clear up things in my own way. You were close to arresting me under suspicious circumstances not long ago. I didn't want that, but a free surrender is different. Well, why don't you put me under arrest? A little while ago you were even offering a big reward for me."

"Mr. Brome Fielding offered the reward, not the police," replied Congreve, after a moment of enigmatic meditation. "Anyhow, Stover, we've changed our minds about you. The finger of suspicion has veered away—"

"Toward Bee MacGowan."

"I answer no questions," said Congreve, thereby admitting that Stover was right, "and I don't commit you to prison. I only desire that you remain in Pulambar. In fact, I'll make sure that you do. Hold out your left hand."

Stover obeyed, and upon the skinned and abraded wrist Congreve snapped a bracelet of the sort Stover had already worn. Carefully the officer fitted the thing, so that it fitted almost as snugly as a noose of cord.

"You seem to have shaken one of these things off," he observed. "You'll not get rid of that one, Mr. Stover. And I don't think I have to tell you about the peculiar and unpleasant properties of this little device. When things cool off, and if you stay in the clear, I want to hear from you just what happened since I saw you last."

"That's a date," agreed Stover. "Now may I see Miss MacGowan?"

"You may not." That was even more of an admission that the police were holding her.

Stover shrugged and left.

He felt that he saw through Congreve's new attitude toward him. Bee MacGowan had become the chief suspect while he, Stover, was only under mild suspicion. Either that, or Congreve had failed to heap up enough evidence to convict Stover. Bee MacGowan had already half-confessed as the murderer. If she proved innocent, Stover in the meantime might do more to convict himself. That was why he was left free within limitations. Clever man, Congreve.

Meanwhile, Bee MacGowan had complicated matters even more than the police considered. Yesterday Stover had escaped brilliantly and daringly. Now he had wanted to surrender, rebelling at the thought of retaining his freedom at the hands of the girl. He told himself this was not a romantic regard for her, but only what any self-respecting male should do.

She was wrong in taking responsibility for the quarrel, the murder, and Dillon Stover's subsequent plight. True, the fight had started over her, but it might have started over any passably attractive girl, Malbrook and Stover being the men they were. Beyond that, Stover wished she had sat tight and let him do the thinking and fighting.

"Strong-headed, but a girl in a million," he estimated her to himself. "No, in a million million. She feels that it's her duty to take the fall, I suppose, but I wish she hadn't surrendered. The charge would be bound to break down against me or any other innocent person."

That new thought flashed like light in his mind. It was a rationalization that must have come to Bee

MacGowan. She had invited arrest and indictment for the sake of giving him freedom—because she was really innocent. She had courage to risk trial on those grounds.

"I believe in her!" he decided. "I'll make the rest believe in her, too. Meanwhile, what am I mooning about? The real killer's swanking around free. I'm supposed to be after him. That," he told himself with all the assurance in the world, "is what she set me free for—to clear us both and punish a cowardly assassin."

He reached a vestibule-restaurant, built like a great glassed-in balcony hanging high on the cliff of the same building that housed Congreve's headquarters. Sitting down at a withdrawn table, he called for a late breakfast and a wireless telephone. Between bites, he contacted Buckalew's apartment. The hired robot servitor answered metallically. Then came the voice of Buckalew.

"Dillon, my boy! Don't tell me where you are—the police are looking everywhere for you."

"Not they," replied Stover. "I just tried to give myself up to Congreve. All he's doing is to hold me close to Pulambar. Bee MacGowan is the one they're working on now."

"I was present when she was arrested," Buckalew informed him.

"So was I," Stover admitted. "Inside the shell of that Martian's robot helper—why gulp like that, Robert?"

"I didn't gulp, Dillon. I never do. So you were disguised as a robot? Remarkable. Only somebody close to your grandfather could have thought of that. As to being held in Pulambar, so am I, the Phogors, Amyas Crofts, and one or two others. If you're not under danger of arrest, Dillon, come home where we can talk more fully."

"As soon as I've finished eating," promised Stover. "I have something of interest to offer, a theory of Bee MacGowan's innocence—there, you gulped again!"

"It was you that time," charged Buckalew. "I heard you plainly. Here, don't ring off yet."

"I heard a click, too," said Stover. "Maybe some third person was tuned in on our wave-length. I'll come to you at once, Buckalew. Wait there for me."

"Take care of yourself," admonished Buckalew.

Finishing his breakfast, Stover sought an outside balcony and hailed a flying taxi. The driver was the same who had served him on the night of the murder. He stared at Stover in astonishment.

"Say," he accused, "the law wants you. There's a reward—"

"Not any more," Stover shut him off. "I'm not on the preferred list at headquarters."

But the driver insisted on a quick radio-phone conversation with police before he would listen to Stover's directions.

Flying back and landing on the balcony of his lodgings, Stover had a sense of unreality, as though he had been gone for months. Enough adventure had befallen him to fill a month, at that. Stover pondered a moment on the relativity of time's passage. Then he went in.

"Robot!" he called. "Get me some fresh clothes. And where's Mr. Buckalew?"

No answer. The front room was dim, but not dark. A couple of lesser radium bulbs still burned. By their light he saw the robot leaning against a wall.

"I gave you an order," said Stover sternly. "Why don't you obey it? Clothes, I said."

The robot did not move. He crossed the floor toward it, putting a hand on its shoulder-joint.

The thing seemed stuck to the wall, as though bolted there. Stover exerted his strength, but could not budge it. He braced the heel of his left hand against the wall to get more leverage, and felt a tug at his wrist. Congreve's bracelet seemed trying to fasten itself beside the robot. Stover jerked away.

"Magnetism. The metal wall's magnetized!" Again he lifted his voice. "Buckalew! Aren't you here? What's going on?"

Turning back toward the center of the room, he saw Buckalew for the first time. His host was seemingly lounging in a corner opposite. Buckalew neither moved nor spoke.

"Don't tell me they've magnetized you, too," cried Stover impatiently. "Speak up, what's happened?"

He took a step toward his friend. At the same time, there was a crash at his elbow. The robot, evidently released from its magnetic bonds, had fallen forward and lay writhing, trying to recover itself.

Stover bent and helped the metal servitor to its flat feet. Then Buckalew's voice was raised in a warning shout that filled the room:

"Look out, Dillon—danger of some kind! *Duck!*"

So startled that he forgot his touchy mystification, Stover released his hold on the robot's arm and again turned toward the corner opposite. Buckalew was falling as the robot had fallen, but more slowly and gently, almost floating downward toward the floor.

"Just what's going on here?" began Stover.

Something dark flashed upon him, seized him and hurled him flat. A moment later, it was as if lightning and thunder had concentrated in the room.

Dillon Stover's senses were fairly ripped out of him.

CHAPTER XI

And Then the Third

STOVER'S hearing came back first; his ears rang and roared. Then his feelings; he ached from head to foot. He opened his eyes to a scene of confusion that still blurred and quivered before him.

"Sit up and drink this," Buckalew was commanding him.

Stover got up slowly. Buckalew fastened a silver collar with one hand, while the other extended a glass.

"Thanks," said Stover, sipping. The drink was full of bite, but it cleared his head and steadied his knees. "How long was I like that?"

"Quite a while. Long enough for me to change my clothes. My others were almost torn off me by the blast." Sure enough, rags of the brown fabric lay on the floor. Stover glanced sharply at Buckalew. Wasn't it a trifle callous of the other to think of dressing before giving aid to an injured man? But Buckalew gave him no opening to complain, gesturing instead to the tumbled furniture and the soot-fogged walls of their once splendid parlor.

"Not quite as powerful an explosion as the one at Malbrook's," went on Buckalew weightily, "or it would have torn off the whole top of this tower, and blown you to atoms."

Stover, swiftly regaining his full strength and sense, now looked down at his own clothes. They were not damaged in the least. Buckalew spoke true words, but enigmatic ones. First of all, how much did Buckalew know about the Malbrook death-blast that he was able so glibly to compare this one with it? Second, why did he speak of Stover only as being "blown into atoms?"

Hadn't he, Buckalew, been in danger as well? Or had he perhaps operated and directed the danger from a position of safety? The thought seemed ungrateful. Buckalew had been the friend of Stover's grandfather, was now the friend of Stover.

"It's got the poor servitor," the younger man made reply, pointing to the shattered mass of metal that had been the robot. "I suppose he got between me and the blast. If so, I can thank a robot for saving me."

"Yes," agreed Buckalew, in a tone that seemed almost bitter. "You can thank a robot for saving you."

"You sound as if you're sorry!" Stover could not help protesting. "Tell me just what happened here. You were here waiting after you answered my phone call. What happened in the meantime?"

"I haven't the slightest idea," replied Buckalew.

"But you must have!"

"I can only say again that I do not. My—my mind went blank."

Stover eyed him narrowly. "You mean, something stunned you?"

"Yes, something like that."

Stover could not see any sign of a cut or bruise upon Buckalew. His hair was as sleek as ever. Only his manner was weary and solemn. Again Stover made a deliberate effort to banish suspicion. He volunteered the story of his recent adventures, finishing with an account of how he had come home to find the robot servitor stuck by magnetic power to the wall and Buckalew himself motionless in a corner.

"I don't remember being in the corner," said Buckalew when he had finished. "I was—overcome in my dressing-room back there. As I remember, I regained consciousness just in time to sense danger and warn you."

"What danger?" Stover demanded. "You knew there would be an explosion?"

If he hoped to startle or trap Buckalew, he was disappointed. The other made steady reply.

"All that I knew was that I had been attacked in some way, and that you had come. After that, the bomb or gun or whatever went off."

They inspected the room, setting up the furniture again and checking damage. Stover ran for a chemical kit, testing the atmosphere that still had a slight murk.

"Old-fashioned nitroglycerin, as in the other case," he announced. "And here, on the floor—"

He knelt in the corner where he remembered seeing Buckalew. There was a stain there. As Girra had done in his presence only a few hours before, Stover made tests. This, too, yielded a trace of synthetic rubber.

Meanwhile, Buckalew was talking on the radio phone.

"No," he was saying, "nothing at all. A trifling accident, no damage. Not worth your notice." He switched off and turned toward Stover. "A police call. Some neighbor gave an alarm."

"Why not call them in?" almost shouted Stover. "Do you want to hide anything from them?"

"Yes. Don't you?" And Buckalew crossed the floor to him. "You want to expose the real murderer by yourself—you told me that. I thought I was helping you."

That should settle suspicions, even if Stover lyingly told himself that he had none. Buckalew continued:

"Undoubtedly the attempt was aimed at you by the real murderer. He will think you destroyed until he hears otherwise."

"But a report to the police, not necessarily public—"

"Have you the slightest doubt that the aforesaid murderer doesn't know everything the police know? For instance, was any public announcement made of your release from the order of imprisonment?"

"No, but we both heard noises that suggested someone listening in on our phone wavelength," reminded Stover, scowling. "That was the probable tipoff."

"Why would an enemy listen in unless he knew you were free and would call me here? No, Dillon. The murderer has access to police records and secrets."

Stover nodded. Buckalew was right. "Then," he announced, "I can limit the suspects to people in pretty high places—the Upper-tower set. People like Malbrook, himself, his partner Fielding, his fiancée Reynardine Phogor, or her stepfather, the Venusian. Or even Amyas Crofts."

"Or me," added Buckalew with the slightest of smiles.

Stover jumped and stared. Buckalew's smile broadened.

"Or me," he repeated. "I'm an old-timer in Pulambar. I have friends and a position. I might be able to get an in at police headquarters. Don't forget that Congreve himself has been conferring with me lately. And I have as good a motive for killing Malbrook as any of the others."

"And a motive for trying to kill me?" asked Stover in spite of himself.

Again Buckalew smiled. "You wouldn't expect me to tell you that, if I wanted to kill you and had failed. Well, to sum up, you have reason to suspect me, and I to suspect you. After all, we were both present when this second explosion was touched off."

"You don't believe in me, then?" demanded Stover.

Buckalew cocked his head, apparently trying to remember something. At last:

"In an ancient but most readable work, called *Alice in Wonderland,* the heroine is addressed by a unicorn. Know what a unicorn is? Well, this one said, 'If you believe in me, I'll believe in you. Is that a bargain?' All right, Dillon, is it?"

He offered his hand. Dillon took it, regretting wholeheartedly that he must make a secret reservation.

"Your little friend Bee MacGowan is cleared by this," Buckalew resumed. "She's in prison even while this murder attempt is made."

"Let's tell the police that," said Stover stepping toward the phone. "They'll release her at once."

"And probably arrest you again," added Buckalew. "Say nothing. She's giving you a chance to clear her and yourself. Use it."

Stover fell into a silence, almost a stupid silence. In the midst of it the front door opened and two figures fairly dashed in. They came to a halt.

"Mr. Stover—er—" stammered the voice of Amyas Crofts.

Stover felt almost grateful for this opportunity to change the subject. He strode across to the gilded youngster, glaring a challenge.

"Why do you rocket in like that?" he growled. "What do you want here?" A light seemed to dawn inside his head and stop the aching. "Perhaps you didn't expect to find me alive?"

The companion of Amyas Crofts had turned to dart out again, but Buckalew, moving with amazing speed, gained the door and fastened it. Then he turned to confront the would-be fugitive. It was the girl with red-dyed hair whom Stover knew as Gerda.

"Let me out," commanded Gerda as from under her cape she whipped an electro-automatic pistol.

Without even lifting an eyebrow, Buckalew seized it and wrenched it from her hand.

"Go there and sit down," he told her, pointing toward one of the least damaged chairs. "You might have shot me just then."

Gerda sullenly obeyed, eyes flashing. Meanwhile Stover waited balefully for Amyas Crofts to explain. "It's this girl," Crofts attempted at last. "Gerda, she calls herself. She came to my apartment, told me she knew that I was crazy about Bee MacGowan, just the same as you are—"

"Never mind who I'm crazy about," snapped Stover, his blood seething. "Your affairs, not mine, are being looked into. Gerda told you that. What next?"

"She said that if I came here I'd see for myself that there was no more reason to think you'd stand in my way with Bee. When I hesitated, she begged me to come. Said she'd come with me."

"He's lying," contributed Gerda from where she sat under Buckalew's guard.

Stover did not know which to believe. He laid a big hard hand on Croft's shoulder. "I've got a mind to knock your teeth out through the back of your neck," he said angrily. "So you busted in here without asking permission."

"Gerda said it was all right, that you were expecting me," explained Crofts, "and keep your hands to yourself. I'm not so sure you could knock my teeth anywhere."

"Gentlemen," interposed Buckalew smoothly, "you're clouding some rather important issues with these personalities. Dillon, I venture to say that one of these visitors, and perhaps both, thought to find us dead."

Crofts's white anger turned to white panic. "Dead?" he repeated. "You think we were going to kill you?"

"He's putting on an act," accused Gerda, and Buckalew waved for her to keep quiet.

Stover had cooled down a trifle, telling himself that the mere mention of rivalry over Bee MacGowan must not be enough to drive him so crazy with wrath. He saw that Crofts wore a bracelet like his. This man, too, would be kept in Pulambar by Congreve for possible further investigation. Let him go, decided Stover, and keep an eye on him.

"Get out," he told Crofts.

The other went to the door, then paused. His eyes gleamed like furnaces. "You're on your own ash-heap," he said. "Some time we'll get together on equal ground."

"Out," bade Stover, "or I'll drop you clear down to the canal level."

Crofts was gone, and Stover walked back to where Gerda sat.

"Buckalew tells the truth. You thought we'd be dead. Why did you come here with Crofts?"

"Because I was paid to," she told him with cheerful irony.

"You mean," prompted Stover, "that you were bringing him here so that he could be framed with the crime?"

"Or," put in Buckalew, "that he was the one who paid you, and you both came to make sure we were dead?"

"That would be telling," Gerda replied to both questions. "Mr. Stover already knows that I'm working for that mysterious blast-killer. I won't deny it. But I'll deny other things. I'm a good servant." She gazed from

one to the other of them. "And those hard looks won't
get you anywhere, either. I know that Mr. Stover won't
hurt me physically, and that he wouldn't let Mr. Buckalew try."

Stover walked to a closet and opened it. There was
barely room inside for a person to stand comfortably.
"We'll lock you up for long enough to think it over," he
said.

With a disdainful smile the girl sauntered across and
into the narrow prison. When he had latched the door,
Stover looked at Buckalew, who had followed him.

"Well, Dillon?" prompted Buckalew in a clear, carrying voice. "You realize that there is no ventilation in
that closet?"

There was plenty of ventilation, but Stover took the
cue.

"Of course not," he agreed. "I count on that to change
her mind. She'll start to smother, and then she'll talk."

Gerda said something profane from inside the closet.

"What if she lies?" asked Buckalew.

"We'll shut her up again," said Stover.

"Watch here," suggested Buckalew. "I'll make a tour
of the rear rooms. We don't know yet what damage has
been done there."

Stover nodded agreement, and sat down in the chair
facing the closet door.

He had not long to wait. Gerda began to pound on the
inside of the metal panel.

"Well?" said Stover.

"Let me out," she pleaded in a tense, muffled voice.

"Ready to tell us what you know?"

"No. I daren't. But—there's something in here with
me!"

Stover laughed. "It's too dark for you to see anything."

"I felt a touch—there it is again." Her voice rose shrilly. "Stay away from me, whatever you are, or I'll smash you!"

The door shook with a deafening boom.

Even before Stover could unfasten the latch, he knew what had happened inside. He flung open the door, and the body of Gerda pitched limply out into his arms.

CHAPTER XII

Fight and Fall

STOOPING, Stover laid Gerda at full length upon the metal floor. Her eyes were shut, and her face completely clear of all cunning and mocking expressions, as if she realized that such things would avail her no longer. She was bruised and the back of her skull was driven in, but there was surprisingly little blood.

"A small explosion," said Stover aloud. "First that shattering one at Malbrook's, then a lesser one in this parlor, and now one quite light in the closet. Robert, come here!"

"I am here," said his friend behind him. "This is a bad mess, Dillon. I suppose you realize that there would be very little chance of clearing yourself now that someone else has been killed in your presence—and a police spy at that."

"Did I tell you she was a police spy, or do you know that as a man-about-Pulambar?" demanded Stover. Then, without waiting for a reply: "All I can say is that I'm innocent."

"And all I can say is that I know you are," Buckalew assured him.

"How do you know?"

"I said once that I'd believe in you,"

Buckalew reminded him gently, "and I meant it. Cover her over with this cloak. Now, to look inside the closet."

They both did so. Stover saw things that had become almost familiar—a murk of pungent nitroglycerine vapor, a stain that would certainly prove to be traces of synthetic rubber. He saw, too, a small hole, a ventilator like the one at Malbrook's, but in a corner of the floor. He poked a finger into it.

"What's below this place, Robert?"

"Why, nothing. Or nearly nothing. This tower is on a framework of steel girders, you know. Nothing below us for hundreds of yards except crisscrossed cables and iron bars."

Stover raced out onto the balcony. Amyas Crofts was not there, nor any moored flying vessel. Stover threw a leg over the barred railing.

"Here, Dillon," called Buckalew anxiously. "What are you up to?"

"I'm going to have a look beneath us," replied Stover. "If I can swing down below just a few feet, I can see clear under from front to back."

"You think the murderer might be down there?"

"I do," said Stover, and swung his other leg over. He was clinging to the railing with both hands, his toes finding a ledge barely two inches wide. He tried to keep his eyes and thoughts from the abyss below. If he fell, he'd bounce off the lower roof and drop into a deep of two miles and more to the canal level.

"Let me go down," offered Buckalew. "You'd better not risk it, Dillon. Ticklish work, climbing around."

Buckalew should have known that such talk would force him to the try, reflected Stover. Perhaps Buckalew did know. The young man's temperament would never let him pause now. Grasping the rail in both hands, he lowered himself a trifle, one foot extended to grope for another toehold.

"If you insist," Buckalew added, "I can help you."

He ran back into the parlor, and brought out a long dark cord of velvet fabric. "This was used to bind the drapes at the windows," he said. "It's strong enough to bear your weight on Mars. Take hold, I'll lower you."

Stover had to accept. Indeed, he could not go down without such help. He gripped the soft, tough cord, and Buckalew began to pay it out.

A dozen feet or so Stover descended like a bucket into a well. There was nothing below save the thin air of Mars, nothing to cling to save this velvet line held above by one he was not sure he could trust. Then he was below the floor-plane of the apartment, looking into an openwork mass of structural metal.

He swung inward, catching a girder in one hand.

"Slack off a little," he called up to Buckalew. "I'm all right. Make the rope fast so that I can swarm up again."

Like a sailor among rigging, Stover worked his way in among the struts, beams and cross-pieces. He found footing upon a horizontal girder, less than ten inches across. A higher and smaller bar of metal served as a sort of hand-rail. He moved in gingerly fashion to a point beneath the closet where Gerda had been overtaken by death.

"Hello!" he exclaimed, though he did not think of anyone hearing him. "Here's something caught just inside. A bit of—"

With the forefinger of his free hand he dug it out of the ventilator opening. It was a bit of elascoid, thin as silk and flexible and stretchy as the finest rubber. The form of it was tubular. It was the size of his forefinger and the length of that forefinger's two upper joints. He sniffed at it and inhaled a pungency like that of the explosive reek. But how could such a limp fragment be a weapon?

He tucked it into a pocket of the stolen tunic he still wore, preparatory to turning carefully around to retrace his steps along the girder.

"Stand right there," came a penetrating whisper.

Stover finished the turn, and looked back the way he had come.

Upon the girder, not five feet away, stood a figure as tall as he, but as vaguely draped as a ghost in a voluminous mantle of neutral gray. Over the head was a loosely folded veil, with no holes for eyes or nose. Apparently it could be seen and breathed through from within. One hand poked from under the robes, heavily gloved. That hand pointed a pistol-form ray thrower straight at the pit of Stover's stomach.

"Stand right there," repeated that genderless whisper. "You have poked too close to an awkward truth, Dillon Stover. Which death do you choose, the hard one or the easy?"

The mention of death did not frighten Stover. Aside from the fact that he had considerable personal courage, he had been in too much danger for the past sixty hours to be much shaken now. But he recognized that his chance of escape and pursuit of his quest had grown slim and feeble. He stood still, tense, watchful, wondering if his already overworked luck would provide him with one more straw at which he, a drowning man, might clutch.

"The hard death," he said, "because it will involve you."

The robed one moved a step closer. Stover heard the clang of heavy metal soles. This person was standing upon stiltlike devices to lend false height.

"Think what you say," came the whisper. "You are asking me to burn you in two with this ray. Better a simple plunge down with quick oblivion at the end."

"Not a bit of it," flung back Stover. "I'm here on Mars for a specific purpose. Two specific purposes. Primarily, to bring water back and turn this poor dried-out world into something like life again. That brought me to Mars, and it's a thing I won't let go of easily. Secondarily," and Stover's voice grew fierce, "there's the job of bringing you to justice. It'll be done."

"It will not be done," came the sneering denial. "You die, here and now. If I burn you with the ray—"

"If you do," finished Stover for his threatener, "my body will drop down and be found below by the police. I'll be set down as a murder victim. Understand? It'll be a clue against you, whoever you are hiding in that fake-melodrama robe. You'll be just a little closer to discovery and destruction. Go on, scorch me with your ray. I'd not ask for mercy even if you were going to cook me to death by inches."

"Wait," said the other. "You are wise, Dillon Stover, in your deductions about me and my intentions. You rouse my admiration. I am tempted to give you a chance for life. A fair fight, eh?"

The gloved hand lifted and gestured, the ray thrower's muzzle went out of line. Stover sprang forward on the girder, forgetting how precarious was his footing and balance, and struck hard with his right fist into the center of that veiled face.

His knuckles felt as if they would explode—the veil also hid some kind of metal visor that helped muffle and disguise the whisper. There was a swirl of draperies as the tall body swayed back before that mighty buffet. But there was no knockdown, no plunge from the girder.

"I hoped that you would strike," came the whisper, exultant this time. "My shoe-soles have magnets, holding me to this metal girder."

Pulling itself erect again, the robed thing clubbed him with the muzzle of the ray thrower.

Stover did not duck quickly enough. A blow glanced on the side of his head. He reeled, and there were no magnetized shoe-soles to save him. He lost his footing, plunged from the girder. Falling past it, he tried vainly to clutch it with his hands.

He was falling headlong. Down below, seen through cross-angled metal bars and cables as through an intricate web, was the distant broad roof that upheld the scaffolding.

"I'm done for," he told himself. "Victim number four of this wild beast of Pulambar. And my body will look like the victim of accident or suicide. Won't even supply a clew."

He struck heavily.

CHAPTER XIII

Half a Key

FORTY feet below the girder, two cables forked from a common mooring, making a narrow, spring-armed V. Into the angle of that V Dillon Stover had fallen. Even on light-gravitied Mars it was a heavy tumble and the impact of Stover's body made the two cables snap apart, then back. He was caught at the waist like a frog caught in the beak of a stork.

Lying thus horizontally, feet kicking and head dangling, Stover wondered whether to be thankful or not. He seized the cables and tried to push them apart, but they were tough and tight-squeezing, and his right hand had sprained itself by striking that veiled metal mask. He relaxed, saving strength. As he did so there was the snarling *snick* of an MS-ray cutting through the air close to him.

He looked up. The draped figure knelt on the girder and levelled the ray thrower at one of the cables. The metal sizzled. Stover's pinched abdomen felt the cable vibrate. Still chary of marking Stover with a telltale wound, the killer above was trying to cut the metal strand that held him and set him falling again.

"I wish you luck!" the young man called, and his swaddled destroyer made a salute-gesture of irony with the ray thrower. Then came a new sound, a whistling, shrieking siren.

Stover looked outward. A plane, a taxi flyer, was hovering and bobbing just beyond the scaffolding. Somehow the drama on the girders had attracted attention. Another plane came, another. The ray above him was shut off.

Stover, cramped and half suffocated, gestured to the pilots of the machines. Pointing to the scissors-like cables that imprisoned him, he spread his hands in appeal for help. One of the planes made a wriggling motion in midair to indicate understanding. But no one seemed to know how to reach and free him.

Stover groaned despite himself. Then, once more a voice from the girder forty feet overhead.

"Dillon, hold tight! I'm going to get you out of that."

It was Buckalew, running along the narrow footpath like a cat on a fence-top. One of his hands flourished a velvet rope.

Stover tried to call back but he had no breath to do more than wheeze and gasp. Buckalew was lowering the rope. It dangled against Stover's hand, and he seized it.

Now he would be pulled up. All the way? Or would Buckalew let him fall, seemingly by accident? Had Buckalew clambered down out of the tower, or had he merely thrown off the gray disguisings? No time to speculate now. Stover caught the velvet strand. It tightened.

But he was too closely crimped, and one of his hands was injured. The first tug wrenched the rope from him, and Buckalew almost fell with the sudden slackening of the cord.

More sirens. The air around the scaffolding was thick with planes. Drivers and passengers were sympathetic and most unhelpful.

"Chin up, Dillon!" Buckalew yelled above the racket. "I'll try something else."

He rove a noose in the rope's end. This he lowered and snared one of Stover's waving feet. Then he began to pull. Stover shifted in the clutch of his trap, but could not be dragged free.

Buckalew sprang backward into space.

He kept hold of the rope, which tightened abruptly across the girder. The sudden application of his hurled weight did the trick. With a final cruel pinch that all but buckled Stover's ribs, the cables released their hold. Then Stover was being drawn up by one foot, his head downward. Buckalew came slowly down at the other end of the rope. The smaller man was strangely the heavier. Drawing to a point opposite Stover, Buckalew caught his friend by the arm.

"Steady on," he bade, twisting the two strands of the line together.

Then, thankfully and triumphantly, Stover and Buckalew climbed hand over hand up the doubled length of velvet. A few moments of rest on the girder, and they walked back along it to where another length of cord gave them a passage back to their own balcony.

To the thronging plane-riders who now closed in, Buckalew had a brief word of dismissal.

"Did you like the show? We're rehearsing an acrobatic turn for next year's society circus on Venus. Not very good yet, are we?"

Then he closed the door behind him. He brought the exhausted Stover a drink, and listened to all that had happened below the floor.

"You say that the disguised one was as tall as you?" he asked at the end of the story.

"Yes, with those false magnetic soles," replied Stover. "He'd have to be built up to be that big. All my suspects are shorter than I am." He measured Buckalew's middling height with his eye as he spoke.

"Why say 'he'?" asked Buckalew. "Couldn't it be a woman, with that whisper, the stilts and draperies. Reynardine Phogor?"

"She might be a killer," admitted Stover. "You seem to think so."

"I didn't say that. I only want her to be remembered. Don't drop any suspects from the list without very good reasons."

"But where could that murderer have popped from?" elaborated Stover. "The whole scaffolding's open-work. Not place enough to hide even a small person. Yet I turned around and there he—or she—was."

"You said the draperies were gray," reminded Buckalew. "A good color to blend in with the metal. Probably the murderer crouched motionless while you walked right past."

Stover shook his head and rubbed his bruised side gently. "I find that pretty hard to accept, on a ten-inch girder."

"You weren't looking for a human figure," persisted Buckalew. "You were looking for clues—by the way, did you find any?"

Stover's hand crept into the pocket of his tunic. His finger touched the scrap of elascoid. Perhaps Buckalew could help him decide exactly what it was. Perhaps, again, Buckalew knew only too well what it was.

"No," he said. "Nothing at all."

Then his eyes had time to quarter the room, and he jumped up quickly.

"Look! Gerda—her body! It's gone!" And it was.

The high-tower set was holding carnival at the Zaarr. The place was packed, nearly every seat and table taken. There was lots of music, and Venusian dancers—frog-women who, grotesque as they were, had yet the grace of snakes. To keep them supple and energetic, a misty spray of water played over the glass stage, water that might cool the parched and dehydrated tissues of many a Martian pauper out on the deserts far away.

Thus in an atmosphere like that of their own foggy planet, the dancers outdid themselves, their gliding gestures moving swiftly in faultless rhythms. Suddenly, with an almost deafening shout, they sprang into the air—and disappeared.

It was a tremendous effect. The water-spray died at once, leaving nothing but luminous air under the play of a pale light. Thunderous applause.

"I know how that is done," Phogor said to his stepdaughter Reynardine. "The atom-shift ray. It strikes any material into atomic silence, so that they fade from view. See, the light is being wheeled away. Those dancers, in the form of invisible atomic clouds, will go with it and re-materialize in the green room. Scientifically simple, and very uncomfortable, I hear, to those involved. But the show must go on. Pulambar demands new thrills."

Brome Fielding smiled, as if he, for one, found the new thrill acceptable. Only Amyas Crofts, in a remote corner, glowered.

For he had been looking toward the main entrance, and had seen the arrival of the two new guests who had just come to occupy the last reserved table.

Dillon Stover, towering and handsome in blue and scarlet, made a commanding figure even in that richly decked crowd. Behind him came Buckalew, more somber but quite as fashionable in black and silver. Where Stover's expression was strained and defiant, Buckalew was absolutely calm and unruffled of feature.

Others saw the pair, and stared as fiercely as Amyas Crofts. The Martian who had replaced Prrala as proprietor fumbled over the admission card. Others, including many guests, glowered at the recently jailed young man who returned so nervily to the very heart of society. And one figure swaggered up, a man in the uniform of a space-officer.

"Now I can believe all I hear of you, Stover," said this person in a thick, disagreeable voice. "Only a man who is all brass and no heart would have the crust to come over here."

He was almost as tall as Stover and heavier. His face might have been boldly handsome before dissipation coarsened it. As he spoke, his right hand slid inside the front of his tunic.

Stover met his stare. "Who are you?"

"Sharp. Captain Sharp. Retired. And," the voice grew nastier still, "since you must have come here just to show us your face—"

Turning from Stover, he addressed the crowd that watched as expectantly as it had watched the encounter with Malbrook three nights before. "This man's crust would blunt a rocket-kick!" he bawled. "Twice a murderer, and he coldly comes here." He turned back to Stover. "What have you done to Gerda?"

"Nothing, if it's any of your business," said Stover, fighting to keep his temper.

The coarse face darkened. "I love her—and she's disappeared. You," he leveled a forefinger, "did away with her. Well, you were full of fight once before here. How about fighting now?"

"Careful, Dillon," warned Buckalew. "He's deliberately making trouble."

"Maybe you'll fight for this!" raged Captain Sharp.

He slapped Stover, open-handed. Then, as before with Malbrook, people were interfering. Among them was one who hadn't been here on the earlier occassion—Congreve. He caught Sharp by the shoulders and thrust him back.

"Don't you High-tower sparks do anything but hit each other?" he asked dryly.

The new Martian proprietor came towards Stover. "I feel, ssirr, that you had betterr go elssewherre. We cannot have ssuch brrawling around here."

"I'm going," growled Stover. "My enemies know I'm still in the running, for lightning to challenge twice in the same place."

They went outdoors, and Buckalew signaled for an air-taxi.

"I've got it!" Stover exclaimed suddenly.

"Got what?"

"The key—half a key, anyway. This is a murder gone wrong. Just now this Sharp tried to force a quarrel on me."

"Probably acting for the murderer," chimed in Buckalew.

"Exactly. It was all fixed up. This Captain Sharp sneers at me and does his best to make a fight of it. That was what Malbrook did. Malbrook's wasn't a chance squabble. He engineered things to make a situation out of which a duel would come. For some reason, I was marked to be murdered."

Buckalew gazed at Stover with what might have been critical wonder in his deep dark eyes. "You may be right. But Malbrook was killed first."

"That's it. First a plot to destroy men. Then someone kills Malbrook instead. I wonder who all are involved."

"I can name one," said Buckalew. "Bee MacGowan."

Stover started and tried to gesture the idea away.

"But she was what you fought over, Dillon," Buckalew pursued. "She was at your table just as Malbrook came over and used her to make a scene. I said once not to forget any single figure in this mess. That goes for Bee MacGowan, as well. Here's our taxi."

Stover nodded, but not as a sign of defeat.

"I'll have the solution inside of another day," he vowed.

CHAPTER XIV

Three Calls at Midnight

CONSIDERING that Captain Sharp had just left the expensive and exclusive Zaarr, the sleeping quarters he sought were shabby. They consisted of two small rooms, little larger than cupboards, in one of the lofty, blocky buildings that underlay the high towers among which he had spent a few hours. He entered the front cubicle, and flung himself down in the one chair.

His coarse face bore the look of one angry and worried.

Almost at once his radio phone buzzed. He approached it as a diver approaches a cold plunge. "Yes," he said into the transmitter, "this is Captain Sharp."

"You have failed me," came a cold whisper he knew.

"It wasn't my fault," Sharp began to plead.

"Do not palter. Do not argue. I was there and saw. You handled the situation foolishly. I felt like telling Mr. Congreve the truth about you, that you're guilty of many offenses against the Space Laws, and letting him carry you off to jail. I am through with you now."

"Give me a chance!" Sharp cried vehemently. "I need that money you offered me. Let me meet Stover again. I promise—"

"Your promises are nothing, Sharp. Less than nothing."

A noise behind. Sharp set down the phone and turned.

The door to the rear room, where his bed was located, swung open. A towering shape in blue and scarlet stepped into the light.

Sharp swore shrilly, and his hand dived into the bosom of his tunic. But Dillon Stover's right hand, its sprained knuckles lightly bandaged, leveled an electro-automatic.

"Freeze," he commanded, and Sharp obeyed. Stover crossed to him and with his left hand drew the weapon that Sharp carried in an armpit holster.

The captain found the spirit to answer. "You aren't going to give me anything like a fighting chance, I suppose."

"You suppose correctly." Stover studied him with his bright blue eyes. "Well, Sharp—Captain Sharp, *discharged*—"

"How did you know that?" wheezed Sharp, badly shaken.

"I looked through your papers while I waited here for you. As to how I got in—you were going to ask that next? I hired the room next to you and cut through the wall with an MS-ray. Your address? I got it at the Zaarr, where all guests are required to register. Why did I come? To settle accounts. That handles everything you're thinking to ask me. Now I'll do the questioning."

"You've got the guns," snarled Sharp. "Ask me whatever you want to."

Stover sat down, but did not grant a similar relaxation to his captive. "You were set on me like a mangy dog," he charged. "To pick a fight and kill me. Who hired you?"

Sharp shook his head. "I can't tell you that."

"You mean you won't?" Stover's eyes narrowed, and the pistol seemed to tense itself in his bandaged hand.

"I can't. I never saw the bird." Sharp was suddenly earnest. "Listen, you must believe that. I saw only a big shape wrapped in a cloak, with the face covered."

"Gray cloak? Veil? Gloves? Was it man or woman?"

Again Sharp shook his head. "I can't say. He—or she—whispered. I couldn't tell a thing about the voice." He glanced furtively around. "I'm risking my life with every word I speak."

"You're risking your life with every word you hold back," Stover informed him. "When were you given this job?"

"Today about noon." Sharp gulped and his voice trembled. "I came to Pulambar a week ago, hoping to make a connection—a space-job."

Stover nodded. He knew how discredited space-men sometimes signed with outlaw vessels in such big, lax communities.

"The job didn't come through," Sharp went on, "and I was pretty desperate. Then about noon, as I say, there was a buzz at my door bell. In stalked this bird in the cloak and veil."

"Asking you to kill me," supplied Stover. "And you agreed."

Sharp spread his hands in appeal.

"I'm broke. I'll starve. Don't I have to live?"

"I fail to see the necessity. And you won't live long if you don't get on with this yarn. Talk fast, and don't lie."

There was no danger of Sharp lying. "I was told that you'd be at the Zaarr tonight—you'd made reservation—and that there'd be an admission card in my name there," he rattled on. "I was told how to pick the scrap by mentioning a woman named Gerda."

"You don't know Gerda?" put in Stover.

"Never heard of her before today." Sharp was almost in tears. "Mr. Stover, all I can say is that I'm sorrier than—"

"You'll be sorriest if you try to fool or forestall me," Stover promised grimly. "And just now, I judge that the whisperer was on your phone."

"Yes, telling me that I'd failed, was through, wouldn't get paid anything."

Stover had relaxed a trifle. Sharp sprang at him. Without rising from his seat, Stover lifted a leg and kicked his assailant in the chest. Sharp fell, doubled up and gasping. Stover laughed shortly, and rose.

"I'm going," he said. "By the way, do you realize your phone never tuned off?"

He stepped to the instrument and spoke into it. "Hello, are you there? . . . I heard the connection break, Sharp. The whisperer's been listening."

Sharp started moaning. "We've been heard. I spilled the dope. Now I'm done for."

"Good night," said Stover, and moved toward the door. Sharp got to his feet. "Wait! What's to become of me?"

"That's problematical, Sharp. I can't do anything. I carry my life in my hand everywhere I go."

"What had I better do?"

Stover thought. Then:

"Go to police headquarters. Look for a special agent named Congreve. Tell him any dirty thing you've done, and it'll land you in a cell. You should be safe there. Later on, I'll get in touch with you. We may make a deal if you'll talk in court."

Reynardine Phogor and her stepfather looked up in irritated wonder as the robot servitors in the reception hall buzzed and rasped in protest. There was a clanking scuffle as a robot was being pushed aside. Then a blue and scarlet giant stalked in.

"Dillon Stover!" exclaimed Reynardine.

Phogor's frog-face was distorted with fury. "What new violence—" he began angrily.

Stover gestured for quiet. "I'm trying to help. About the murder of Malbrook and its effect on you."

The girl drew herself up. She was magnificently dressed, with a little too much sparkle. Her fine eyes glittered disdain. "How can you help?" she demanded.

"By turning up the real murderer. That would help you—unless one of you did it." Stover looked at each in turn. "Don't call any robots, Phogor. They'll get smashed all out of working order. Listen to what I have to say, and then I'll go."

Phogor and Reynardine looked at each other. Then: "Say what you wish," granted Phogor.

"It's about this alleged will," said Stover. "You, Miss Reynardine, are very confident of its existence."

She nodded her head, and the light played on its onyx streakings. "I am confident. That is, unless Brome Fielding destroyed it."

"You saw the will?"

"I heard it. You see, it's a televiso record, picturing Mace announcing his bequests verbally. In it he recognized me as his intended wife, and considers me his principal heir-at-law."

"Perfectly legal," seconded Phogor in his mighty voice.

"Would he have kept the will in his fortified room?" asked Stover. "If he did, it's probably destroyed. Everything was smashed by the explosion."

"That may have happened," sighed Reynardine, as though she disliked to shift the blame for the will's loss from Fielding.

Stover asked one more question. "You hate Fielding, Miss Reynardine?"

"That is an insolent remark," began Phogor, but his stepdaughter waved him to silence.

"Why not tell Mr. Stover? All the rest of Pulambar seems to know. Mr. Fielding wants to marry me."

"Oh," said Stover. "And has he ever suggested marriage or made love before?"

She shook her head. "He doesn't put it on an emotional basis. Says that he and I were the closest two persons to Mace, and that we should marry because of that relationship. Rather fantastic. And," she smiled a little at Stover, "I don't find him attractive."

"I think Mr. Stover's unwarranted inquisition has gone far enough," contributed Phogor. "We are both tired. We have been frank. Let him be considerate, and leave us."

Stover bowed, and left.

In the reception hall that had been Malbrook's, Congreve and Fielding faced each other above the body of Gerda.

"Thank heaven I asked you to come with me," said Fielding, shaken.

Congreve looked at the corpse again. "It would have been hard to frame you with this. She's been dead for hours. Now tell me again."

"A radio phone call. A whispering voice told me to come here alone. But I had the inspiration, a lucky one, to ask you to come with me. You say this was one of your undercover people? Was she working on this murder case?"

Someone else entered. It was Stover, who gave only one look at Gerda. To Fielding he said: "They told me at your place you'd come here."

"Get out," Fielding said.

"No," demurred Stover. "I'm in this case up to my neck. Mr. Fielding, do you love Reynardine Phogor? Did you ask her hand in marriage?"

"You're insolent." That was Congreve, not Fielding. "You're officious, too. And you're still under suspicion."

"I know that," said Stover. "That's why I want to help."

"Leave it to the police," snapped Fielding. "I ought to demand your arrest now, Stover. Get out, I say."

Stover turned to the door. "Tonight," he said over his shoulder, "I've stood face to face with the murderer of Mace Malbrook."

It was hard to say which started the most violently, Congreve or Fielding.

Stover laughed, and was gone.

CHAPTER XV

Captain Sharp

"PSSST! Mr. Stover!"

Dillon Stover, stepping out on the balcony of Malbrook's old quarters, stopped in the very act of summoning a flying taxi. He looked in the direction of the muttered signal.

At one end of the balcony was a service stairway. Upon that stairway, at a level so that only his head and shoulders were exposed, stood someone whose outline in the gloom was vaguely familiar. "This way, Mr. Stover!" He turned and approached, cautiously. Four days of desperate action, of chasing and being chased, had made Stover give much attention to every possibility of danger. If this was an assassin he was going to be sorry.

But the man who had hailed him turned and ran swiftly and furtively down the stairs. Stover followed, his body tense and ready for any sort of action—to fly, to strike out, to beat off an attack. No such need came. The two men gained a balcony below Malbrook's, and here Stover came close enough to recognize his companion.

"Captain Sharp!"

"I c-came here because—"

Stover waved away the words. "You're in danger, Sharp. Mortal danger. I warn you, not because I value your precious carcass, but because you may be able to give evidence for me. Your best chance is to do what I told you. Go and confess some minor crime and get locked up in the police detention cells."

Sharp shook his head furiously. "I found that I can't do that. There's too much fire on me."

The man, for all his coarseness, had appeared strong to Stover at the earlier meetings. Now he seemed ready to crumble, to collapse. His considerable size made him the more unwieldy in the grip of whatever terror had him.

"You see," Sharp continued, "the whisper-voice got back on the phone again after you were gone and I was making ready to leave. That fellow, whoever he was, had heard plenty. He said that the police were being warned about some real dirty things I'd done—killings."

"And so you can't face the music?" finished Stover for him.

"Not when it plays that sort of tune."

"It's playing the Dead March now," Stover informed him grimly. "Well, so you came to me. How did you know I was here?"

"I didn't. I came here after I heard at Mr. Brome Fielding's place he'd headed this way. But when I found that a police officer was with him—"

"Why are you so anxious to see Brome Fielding?" Stover interrupted.

"Because he's the partner of Mace Malbrook. Because he wants to clear up the murder. Because he's got enough influence to hide me and guard me, if I can convince him it's worth his while."

There was the whirr of rockets above. Sharp stepped to the balcony and looked upward.

"The police flyer's leaving," he reported, "with only that cop in it. Fielding's still up above. Let's go talk to him."

Stover put out a hand to stop Sharp, but the captain was already heading for the stairway. Stover followed him. Their heads rose into view of the upper balcony. Fielding stood there, elbows on the railing, looking moodily skyward. At that very moment, an air-taxi curved in and hovered.

"Is that you, Dillon?" asked a voice from inside. Buckalew!

"No," replied Fielding sourly, "it is not."

Buckalew was leaning out of the taxi, but turned to address the pilot: "You say you brought him here, and left him?"

"Yes, sir," answered the man who had flown Stover to the spot some time before. "He told me to go. Said he'd be here for the night."

"Let me assure you that he won't be here for the night," snapped Fielding. "I myself ordered him away."

"Very well," said Buckalew in the placating tone Stover had heard him use before this when conversing with Fielding. The taxi departed.

At once Sharp spoke, in the same tone and almost the same words with which he had attracted Stover's attention: *Pssst!* Mr. Fielding!"

Fielding spun away from his pose of meditation. One hand whipped an electro-automatic from somewhere. "Who's that?" he demanded breathily. "Show yourself!"

Sharp lifted his hands, and came up the stairs. "It's nobody you really know, Mr. Fielding," he fawned. "My name's Captain Sharp. I wanted to ask you something."

"But you know me," put in Stover, walking up behind Sharp. "As you say, you ordered me off the place. But I'm not taking orders from you just now. In fact, Fielding, here's one point on which we may even collaborate. I mean Sharp here."

Fielding did not put away his gun. "What's this about?" he grumbled.

"Sharp's a witness in this murder case," Stover informed him. "It began when—"

He paused. How much should he tell this professed enemy of his? Fielding spoke carelessly, solving the problem for him.

"Any evidence had better be given to the police. I'm not as officious about this murder as you are, Stover."

"Not to the police yet," interposed Sharp. "I've got a bad record. But maybe, if I showed up when the time was right, with evidence I could give—"

Fielding seemed to understand. "And I'm to give you a hiding place, eh?" he suggested. "Well, maybe it's my duty. Come over to the other end of the balcony, my flyer's there. You can come, too, Stover."

They entered the car. It was a luxurious one, softly and richly cushioned, most of its hull glassed in. Fielding took the pilot's seat, a high-backed metal construction to which, as regulations in Pulambar ruled, a parachute was fastened. He buckled the safety belt across his middle and took the controls.

"Sit here next to me, Stover," he commanded. "Sharp, make yourself comfortable in the rear. I can trust you better than Stover. You're only a petty adventurer of some kind. He's a murder suspect."

This with a sneer. Stover swallowed it with difficulty and took the benchlike chair where a co-pilot generally sat. Like Fielding, he buckled on the safety belt. Fielding dropped into a cushioned chair behind him. The rest of the cabin was dim, with several other seats and lockers. The flyer took off.

"Where to, sir?" asked Sharp, as though he were flying the craft and asking for directions.

"My quarters, across town," was the reply. "There's a

place for you both to stay."

"Both?" repeated Stover. "You aren't offering to put me up, Fielding?"

"I'm telling you that you're staying with me. The police haven't pinned anything to you, but just now, with this shabby Captain Sharp as a helper, you look a trifle riper for—"

"But you were going to guard me at your place, not turn me over to the law!" cried Captain Sharp.

So strident was his cry of protest that Stover turned to look at him. He saw Sharp rising half out of his seat, hand flung forward in appeal—saw, too, in the shadows of the cabin another human figure. The head and shoulders seemed to hunch and expand, the face looked blank and colorless.

Thinking of it afterward, Stover realized that he had been made furtive by the constant thrusting upon him of danger. At the time he thought and diagnosed not at all. He threw off the safety strap and hurled himself out of his seat on the co-pilot's bench, and flat on the floor so that the metal bench was between him and whatever was lurking in the cabin.

"Fielding!" he yelled as he hit the floor. "Sharp! Danger—someone in here with us."

Fielding, too, glanced back. His face writhed.

"You saw—that—" he was trying to form something. His hands fumbled strangely at the controls.

An explosion tore their vehicle to bits. Stover's hearing sense, even while it was shocked and deafened, sorted out the rending of fabric, the starting of joints, the crash of tough glass. He heard, too, the brief half-scream which was all that Sharp had time to utter before destruction overtook him.

His prone position, in a narrow nook between bench and control board, saved Stover. He was not thrown out, though the lower half of the flyer—all that remained intact—turned a complete flop in the high air over Pulambar. He saw the metal pilot's seat go bounding away, Fielding hanging limp in the safety strap. Would the attached parachute open in time to save Fielding?

Stover had no time to watch. For the wreckage, with him wedged among it, was falling into an abyss.

It struck a wire-woven festoon of walk-ways and communication cords between two towers. The wires, though parting, broke the downward plunge a little. Stover managed to writhe along toward the controls. He got his hands on the keyboard, manipulating it frantically. The thing worked. A crippled blast went *pup-pup-pup,* but there was no stopping the awful plunge.

Stover saw the lower building-tops charging up at him, saw too the silvery expanse of a great pool of water that, set among colored lights, did duty as a public square. If he could only land in that. The gravity of Mars was less than Earth's, the fall was consequently slower.

He clutched again at the controls.

The blast, not enough to check the fall, could change the position of the hurtling slab of wreckage. He leveled it out. As he had dared hope, the thing swooped slantwise in its fall. It was approaching the pool at a fearful clip, but not vertically. Before he knew whether to rejoice or despair the shock came, bruising and breathtaking of impact.

The heavy wreck sprang upward like a flat rock skimming along the surface, and Stover was thrown clear at last. High he flew, and down he came, head first. Somehow he got his hands into diving position. Then, with a mighty splash, the only lake of water on all Mars received his body safely.

CHAPTER XVI

Malbrook's Archives

STOVER struck the bottom of the lake with almost un-impeded force, but it was soft. Turning around upon it, he let himself float to the top. It was cool, damp, restful. His head broke water, and he lay low between the ripples, washing the bottom-mud out of his curls and taking stock of the situation.

The walks along the rim of this pool were lined with noisy sight-seers, all gazing to a distant point in the center of the water. Great turmoil showed there, and several light flying machines hovered and dipped above the spot where the wreckage had sunk. Stover struck out for the nearest walk.

"Help me out!" he called to those gathered there, and half a dozen hands reached down to hoist him up.

"What was that splash?" he demanded, to head off any questions and surmises. "It knocked me right off into the water."

"You ought to sue somebody," advised a bystander. "Some fool's flying car came down out of control, it looked like. I just had a glimpse. Come and have a drink to warm you up."

"Thanks, no. I'll get an air-taxi back to my own place," said Stover.

He sought an elevator that took him to a rooftop where several taxis loitered. One of them had a heater inside, and in it Stover deposited himself, directing the pilot to take him for a leisurely tour while his clothing dried somewhat. At length Stover gave the address of Malbrook's fateful apartment.

It would be empty now—or would it?

Buckalew had come to Malbrook's balcony, looking for Stover. He had known that Fielding was there, that Fielding had a moored aircraft. What then?

Stover's mind went back to the happenings of the morning. Buckalew had been absent from the parlor when Gerda was killed in the closet. Later had come evidence that the explosion was engineered from below by some strange elascoid device. And then the assault by the draped figure. Later, the mysterious being was gone, while Buckalew had hauled Stover up from his painful lodgement between those forked cables. Buckalew had been magnificent then. Resourceful, strong, heroic—but mysterious.

"But if he'd wanted to kill me," reflected Stover, "he couldn't have done it then. Too many curious flying folk hovering around. Later, at noon, Sharp seems to have been visited by the same draped whisperer I saw. Was Buckalew with me at that time? I can't remember."

He counted the dead in his mind. First Malbrook, then Gerda, then Sharp. And perhaps Fielding. He himself had almost been added to the list. And, for all his struggles, he was still far from the solution.

"Here's your place, sir," the pilot broke in on his thoughts swung in to Malbrook's deserted and darkened balcony.

"Have you an extra radium torch?" asked Stover. "If so, I'll buy it. Thanks, that's a good one."

He paid for the torch, the journey and the heater, adding a handsome tip. Then he dismounted to the balcony. Letting the taxi fly away, he entered the now deserted and lightless hall where once before he had stricken

Brome Fielding down and had knocked at a door that forthwith blew off in his very face.

He turned on the radium torch he had bought. That same door was partially repaired now, rehinged and fastened to the jamb with a great metal seal. Stover studied that seal. It was fused to the place where the lock had been, and marked with an official stamp. Police had put it in place to keep out meddlers like himself.

But Stover had come prepared. In his tunic pocket was a small ray projector that had survived the fall and the soaking. Drawing it and turning it on, he rapidly melted away the seal. He flung open the door with a creak and entered the blasted apartment.

Plainly it had not been touched since last he had stood inside it, disguised as a robot, with the Martian mechanic Girra. By the light of his radium torch, he began to make a new inspection. The clascoid stain was still on the floor near the half-detached ventilator device.

Stover looked at it once again, then turned his attention to the metal-plated walls. He tapped them once, then again, at regular intervals. They gave a muffled clank, indicative of their massive construction. So he progressed along for a space. Then, on the rear wall, the clank sounded higher, more vibrant—almost a jingle.

"The plating's thin," decided Stover, and brought his torch close to see.

He found no visible juncture, and resumed his tappings. By then he defined a rectangular hollow within the wall, about ten inches by fourteen. A hiding hole, cleverly disguised.

Again Stover plied his light, and this time he made a discovery. The wall at that point had been lightly coated with metallic veneer, the exact tint and shade of the wall. Under it the joinings of the wall cupboard would be hidden. Why, and by whom?

Not Malbrook, Stover decided at once. That cupboard had been devised for his use, probably his constant use. Then someone who had been here since the explosion wanted to seal and hide the place until later, when the guilt was fixed.

"Yes, fixed on an innocent man," decided Stover wrathfully. "Then, with the police away, the hole could be opened and whatever's inside taken out."

He cut the beam of his ray until it would gush out as narrow as a needle and as hot as a comet's nose. Carefully he sliced through the tempered metal of the wall-plate, along the edges of the hollow rectangle. The piece of thin metal fell out. He caught it before it clattered on the floor, and set it carefully down. His torch turned radiance into the recess he had exposed.

Not much within, only a sheaf of papers and a round thing like a roll of gleaming tape. He studied it first. It looked like the sound track of a film, or a televiso transcription. Reynardine Phogor had said that Malbrook's will was in such a form. Was this the will, or something to do with it?

He saw that one edge of the strip was mutilated, as if roughly cut away. And it had been hidden here, in what was the safest hiding place in all Pulambar until someone like himself came with a clue and an inspiration.

Pocketing the little roll, Stover turned his attention to the papers. At the top of the first was a title in big capitals:

CONFIDENTIAL REPORT
KISER DETECTIVE AGENCY
ST. LOUIS, MO.

"Here, I know about that Kiser crowd," Stover told himself at once. "Political outfit—shady work—do anything for enough money. A high-class phony like Malbrook would use just such a detective outfit. But what's a Pulambar biggy doing with shyster sleuths clear across space in St. Louis?"

Just below, in the written report, was the answer to that:

Replying to your inquiries: Dr. Stover's death laid to natural causes. He was old, overworked. One or two thought he went suddenly. Nobody takes such theory seriously.

No information to be had on his condensation experiments. Work said to be almost complete.

His grandson, Dillon Stover, has been trained to same career and is to continue where Dr. Stover left off. Young Stover on survey trip to Mars. Will visit Pulambar.

There, Stover realized, was the motive for the murder that never was committed—his own. Malbrook had grown rich from the monopoly of water rights on this desert world. The condenser ray would make rain possible, spoiling the monopoly and biting into Malbrook's fortune, the fortune Reynardine Phogor now thought to acquire. Malbrook, therefore, had determined to get Stover out of the way, keep him from completing the work.

Stover put the papers into an inside pocket, and turned off his torch. All in the dark he drew himself to his full height.

"But it was a double stalk, and a double plot," he told himself once again. "While Malbrook was after me, somebody was after him. I was nominated for the position of convicted murderer. Now it's gone beyond that, and I'm to be killed to keep my mouth shut. In other words, I must be close to the solution."

Noise in the reception hall just outside. Then a light, a torch like Stover's. It sent a searching ray into the room, centering here and there, finally hovering at the recess Stover had opened. The light shook, as if the hand that held it was agitated. Then it quested again, and its circle fell upon Stover.

His eyes filled with glare, blinding him. He heard a smothered gasp, and sprang in that direction. An electro-automatic spoke, the pellet whining over his head. Then he was upon the newcomer. The pistol flew one way, the radium torch another. The battle boiled up in the dark.

Hard fists clouted Stover on the temple and the angle of the jaw, and his own hands were momentarily tangled in the folds of a flying cloak; but he leaned into the storm of blows as into a hurricane, and got his arms clamped around a writhing waist. Bringing forward a leg, he crooked it behind his adversary's knee and threw himself forward. His weight was not much on Mars, but it was enough. Down they went, Stover on top.

"You were going to rub me out, eh?" he taunted the writhing, flurrying shape he had pinned down.

Only pantings and rustling answered him. His adversary was saving every bit of breath for the struggle. Again a fist struck Stover on the nose, jolting tears into his eyes, but he worked his hands to a throat and fiercely tightened his grip. Fingers tore at his wrists, but they were not strong or cunning enough to dislodge that strangle hold. Stover felt fierce exultation flood him.

"You tried to kill me," he gritted. "Now I'll kill you."

At that moment, more light burst from the front of the hall.

"Reynardine," boomed Phogor. "You slipped out alone, but I guessed you'd come here after the will. I followed."

As his radium flare flooded the place with glow, Stover sprang up and back, he gazed anxiously at his late adversary.

It was Reynardine Phogor, rumpled and half-fainting, her hands at her throat.

CHAPTER XVII

The Roundup

"WHAT does this mean?" Phogor demanded, in the voice of a thunder spirit. He carried a pistol with which he threatened Stover.

Reynardine sat up. Gasping and choking, she managed to speak. "This man was hiding here, knowing that I would come, so that he could attack me.

"Knowing you would come?" echoed Stover sharply. "How would I know that? It was you who attacked me—firing with your pistol."

"You said that the will would be hidden here," she charged. "My stepfather knew that I would head for this place. Undoubtedly you knew the same. And it was you who attacked. I fired in self-defense."

That last was quite true. Stover felt abashed and angry with himself. Yet he did not bring himself to apologize.

"I did not know it was you. I thought it was a man," he explained.

"Daughter, did he hurt you?" Phogor asked. "Because if he did—"

"Careful," broke in Reynardine, who was suddenly the calmest of the three. "His body would be a bad piece of evidence against you. Otherwise, it would give me great pleasure to see you shoot him."

Stover was examining his sprained hand which ached after the scuffle. He hoped devoutly that he had done his last fighting for the night, at least.

"Let me explain one simple item of the business," he attempted. "I know little or nothing about the will. When you mentioned it at your own place, I asked if it might be here. I didn't say it was here. Indeed, I had no way of telling. Perhaps we've both jumped at conclusions, Miss Reynardine."

"You are clever at explanations, Stover," Phogor bellowed at him. His great frog-mouth was hard-set and cruel, and he glared yellowly out of his blob eyes. "I intend to escort you to the headquarters of Congreve. He will thank me for this evidence against you."

"But," returned Stover hastily, "he won't fail to ask what you were doing here."

Reynardine looked at her stepfather. "This man is a savage and perhaps a criminal, but he speaks the truth," she said. "It had better not be known that you and I came here tonight."

Phogor shrugged his shoulders in acceptance of that. To Stover he said: "This means that I won't injure or detain you unless you do something to force action. But you have struck and injured my daughter. That won't pass without some retaliation on my part later. Now I give you leave to go."

"I don't need leave from you to go," retorted Stover, and strode away toward the balcony.

Feet hurried after him. It was Reynardine.

"Mr. Stover," she breathed, "I've been catching back my wind and collecting *my* wits all these past few moments. And, though it was I who got the slamming and choking, I feel less upset about it than my stepfather. For one thing," and she was able to smile quite graciously, "I shouldn't have suggested that you were a criminal. I don't really think you're guilty."

"I know I'm not guilty," he returned, "but with everything so complicated and mysterious, how can anyone else be sure about me—except the actual murderer of your fiancé?"

Phogor approached, furious again. "You dare to insinuate that my daughter is guilty?"

"Mr. Stover is insinuating nothing," Reynardine calmed the Venusian. "He came here to search for evidence, just as we did. And he is more unselfish. We want the will; he only wants a clue to the murder."

"I'm being selfish, too," Stover assured her, for something bade him be loath at accepting favors from her. "I jammed myself into a situation where I must solve this case or be the next victim, or maybe the victim after the next. Well, Miss Reynardine, you're being very kind. But what does this all mean? Why this sudden new attitude on your part?"

"I don't know," she said. "I think I trust you because you're the best-built tall man I ever saw, and with the bluest eyes. Yes," she continued, touching her throat, "and with the strongest hands. I'm able to testify that you fight both hard and fair."

Phogor snorted like a horse in a rainstorm. "This, daughter, is ridiculous. You know nothing about this man Stover."

"Only the things I have just said," she replied to her father, but with her brilliant eyes still on Stover. "I intend to learn more about him."

Stover's reaction to this almost aggressive demonstration of approval was one of baffled suspicion. He doubted if he was of such character and attraction as to sweep this proud and artificial beauty so completely off her feet. Looking at her, he knew that she could be a dangerous person if she dared to use her charm. Like a saving vision came the thought of Bee MacGowan, still in prison that he might have a chance to clear himself and her, too.

"You leave me embarrassed, Miss Reynardine," he said. "So much so that I'll have to say good-night and depart."

"Wait," she said. "Why don't we come with you to your place and talk this thing out?"

"Talk it out?" he repeated. "Well, come on. I'll signal for a taxi."

Buckalew was waiting in the parlor as Stover let his self-invited guests in. One of Buckalew's hands held a fluttering gray cloth, the mantle that had cloaked the figure Stover had met on the girders. With an exclamation, Stover snatched it and looked at it.

"Where did this come from?" he demanded.

"I found it hidden in a corner of the balcony," replied Buckalew. "Probably the one who wore it dropped it there and hopped aboard one of the fleet planes that came around to investigate. I also found the wiring that was used to magnetize the walls. But who are these people?"

"You know them. Miss Reynardine Phogor and her stepfather. They seem to feel that a round-robin discussion will clarify some points of the Malbrook case."

"Perhaps they're right," said Buckalew. "Will you all sit down?"

Reynardine drew herself up in queenly fashion. "I won't sit down," she said. "Mr. Stover, I persuaded you to bring me here because I think you got something to-night that I mean to have—the transcription that embodies the will of Mace Malbrook."

He looked into her searching eyes. "What makes you think that?"

"Because, just before our little struggle, my torch showed me a wall-cupboard that had been rayed open. Nothing in it. Well," she held out her hand, "give it to me. Father, if we have to be violent here it will be easier explained than at poor Mace's old lodgings."

"That is quite right, daughter," agreed Phogor as he drew his pistol. "I think you were clever to switch the scene of action here. Now, if you please, Mr. Stover."

"Hold on!" cried Stover hotly, his temper rising. "I'm handing nothing over to you."

"That," said Reynardine Phogor, "is an admission that you have something." She turned to her stepfather. "If he won't hand it over, take it from him."

Buckalew turned swiftly to a side-table and snatched open a drawer. But before he could dart his hand into that drawer, Phogor fired a pellet that knocked the side-table flying across the room. Out of the drawer fell a small handsome electro-automatic.

"No weapons, Mr. Buckalew," cautioned the Venusian deeply. "You had better stay out of this altogether." To Stover he said: "I give you one more chance, Mr. Stover, to give me whatever you found at Malbrook's."

"Stover will do nothing of the kind," spoke the stern voice of Congreve.

The police head had come in, all uninvited and unnoticed, and had heard most of what had led up to the tense situation. He, too, held a drawn pistol. He extended his free hand.

"I take it you've finally got evidence," he told Stover. "Well, hand it over. This isn't an amateur with a society gun, young fellow. It's a police officer. Quick!"

Stover sighed in resignation and drew forth the papers he had found. Congreve accepted them with a nod, moved back and looked through them quickly.

"Better than I thought," he commented. "Here's the definite proof."

Stover took a step toward him. Congreve tried to put away the slip of paper, but Stover spied some words on it.

Mr. Malbrook:

I did what you said to do about Dr. Stover. Now I want pay, or you'll be just as dead . . .

"Who wrote that?" demanded Stover, walking right up to the muzzle of Congreve's weapon.

"As if you didn't know," Congreve grinned harshly. "It's signed. And the man who signed it is dead tonight."

"I didn't have time to look at everything in that sheaf of notes," Stover assured him. "If it was written by—"

"You know whom it was written by. They just fished him out of the water." The grin vanished. "What was left of him and Brome Fielding's flying car."

Sharp! It had been Captain Sharp, then, who had brought his grandfather to death—and at the orders of Mace Malbrook. Congreve saw knowledge dawn in Stover's face, and chuckled. The police head plainly enjoyed a dramatic situation.

"You want to make a statement and save everybody trouble?" he said. "Let me help you. Sharp was hired to kill your grandfather. You met him at the Zaarr. You quarreled. Later—"

"You're crazy!" exploded Stover. "I'd have gladly killed both Malbrook and Sharp if I'd known they were guilty of murdering my grandfather. He was an asset to the universe, while they were liabilities. But I didn't know, and someone else killed them."

Reynardine Phogor spoke up hurriedly.

"I can vouch for Mr. Stover. He has been with me almost all evening since leaving the Zaarr."

Phogor and Buckalew stared at the girl. Stover laughed.

"Well tried, Miss Reynardine," he jibed. "You want Congreve to leave me here with you, so that you can find out what else I know about this case, at pistol-point, eh?" He addressed the officer again. "If you please, Congreve."

He was about to offer Congreve all the bits of evidence he had collected—surmises, secrets, brief glimpses, the bit of elascoid fabric, everything. But Congreve was so intent on something he had to say that he took no notice.

"Since Stover won't make an admission, it remains to convict him. He is right in making a last-ditch stand of this. Someone may bob up yet as the guilty one. But I want all concerned to come along with me."

"Come where?" asked Buckalew.

"To Brome Fielding's quarters."

"Brome Fielding's!" cried Stover, his voice shaking in spite of himself. "Is he—"

He had almost asked if Brome Fielding had survived that plunge out of the wrecked car. He broke off in time, and Congreve unwittingly answered the question for him.

"Fielding has found the will of Mace Malbrook in a safe at the office they both shared. Since everybody here is mixed up in the murder somehow, I want you to sit in on the hearing of it. We'll pick up Amyas Crofts and go right now."

CHAPTER XVIII

The Testament of Mace Malbrook

THE room was dim as they entered it, dim and quiet, with chairs for all and a blank televiso screen against the rearmost wall. Two figures sat in a corner behind some radio apparatus with a projector attached. One of these stood up and spoke. It was Brome Fielding.

"Phogor and Reynardine," said Fielding, "take these two chairs in the center. Buckalew, sit just behind Miss Reynardine. Congreve, you're here to investigate and protect. Maybe you'd like to sit next to the door, where you can keep an eye on everybody? Mr. Crofts, you may take the chair on the other side of the door. Mr. Stover," and Fielding's voice became an unpleasant growl, "I suppose you're to be congratulated from escaping from that wreck."

"You didn't expect me to live through it?"

"As a matter of fact, I rather did. It was myself that surprised me by surviving. Thank all the gods of all the planets for that automatic parachute."

"You two are talking in riddles," said Congreve coldly. "Better tell me the answers."

"I'll explain fully when we've had the will," promised Fielding. "Probably you'll be glad to hear the whole truth about that accident which you tell me finished poor Sharp. Sit next to me, Stover."

"Why next to you?" asked Stover.

"Because I don't trust you. I want to keep watch over you."

"Isn't Congreve here to do the watching?" mocked Stover.

Amyas Crofts said: "Put Stover next to me, and turn off the lights. Once he threatened me."

Stover looked at Fielding, then at the silent, hulking figure that sat half-hidden behind the radio machinery.

"My bodyguard," volunteered Fielding, as he saw the direction of Stover's glance. "I hired him at once when I heard that you were still alive."

"Not very complimentary to the police," rejoined Stover. "Well, if he's an honest bruiser, let him sit between us. I don't think I trust you, either."

Fielding was silent for a moment. Then: "Not a bad idea. Lubbock, will you trade chairs with me and keep watch over Mr. Stover? If he acts strangely at all, you will know what to do."

The bodyguard made no reply, nor did he move until Fielding put a hand on his shoulder. Then his great hulk shifted smoothly to the chair nearest Stover. Fielding switched off the last dim light, and they heard him fumbling with the controls of his machinery.

"This is a televiso representation, with transcribed sound track," he announced in the gloom. "It depicts the verbal making of the last will and testament of my partner, the late Mace Malbrook."

A click, and the screen lighted up.

They all saw the image of Mace Malbrook, in full color. He sat beside a table on which was placed a microphone to pick up his voice. In one hand he held a glass that seemed to be full of *guil.* A powerful drink, thought Stover, to be sipped while he recorded an important legal document.

Malbrook's pictured face looked pale and sardonic, and his mouth was set in the tightest of smiles.

"My name," came his formal voice, "is Mace Malbrook. The date, Earth time, is May eighteenth, twenty-nine hundred and thirty-six."

"May eighteenth!" breathed Stover. It was the day on which he had come to Mars, the day before the night in which Mace Malbrook had died. Malbrook's voice went on:

"The extent of my property holdings and controls can be ascertained by consulting the public records of the community of Pulambar. I make this statement at this time, recognizing that I may possibly come to my death at the hands of one Dillon Stover."

Stover heard a sigh from someone, perhaps Reynardine Phogor. He divined, rather than saw or heard, a leaning forward of Congreve. In the mind of the police head, Stover's guilt was again confirmed, though probably Malbrook had said what he had said simply in looking forward to a duel. Again the voice of the dead man:

"In the event of my death, I request that this recording be properly observed by my two heirs-at-law, Brome Fielding and Reynardine Phogor; and they be accompanied by reputable and responsible witnesses."

That was the usual introduction to a will so recorded. The image of Malbrook sipped from the glass, and the voice added:

"I hearby make definite statement that, although each of these two heirs expects to receive at my death the overwhelming bulk of my holdings and interests, I am obliged to neglect one of them in order to treat the other as I consider deserved. I now make my formal bequests and decrees. First: That all my debts be paid, and a funeral service be conducted for me in a manner befitting one of my standing and reputation. Second—"

A break in the speech. The figure of Malbrook rose from its seat, as if to lend emphasis to what would follow.

"Second," came words in a louder and sterner voice, "I direct that my former partner, Brome Fielding, be arrested, and charged with my wilful murder for his own selfish profit!"

Loud, raucous confusion. With a loud buzz and snap, the radio mechanism shut off and the screen darkened. But the voice of Dillon Stover rang on the air that still vibrated with the accusation.

"Let nobody move!"

Stover was on his feet, near the door where sat Congreve and Amyas Crofts. He flashed on his radium torch, which he had never put aside since his adventure at Malbrook's, and it filled the room with brightness. It showed all the others risen, all but the mantled bodyguard Fielding had called Lubbock. Fielding himself had moved back from the radio controls, toward a blank-seeming wall.

"Don't try to duck through any hidden panel, Fielding," warned Stover, and his free hand whipped out his ray thrower. "Someone turn on the room lights ... Thanks, Congreve. Now, while Fielding is still pulling himself together, let me say that I pulled a trick to get this case out in the open, and it's succeeded. I added my voice to that of Malbrook. Fielding murdered his partner and the others, for the reason you have just heard. He wanted all of Malbrook's holdings for himself. And he tried to lay the blame on me."

"Mr. Stover—" began Congreve angrily.

"Don't interfere now," spoke up Buckalew suddenly and clearly. "I respect the law, but not all the decisions of all its representatives. Stover must be allowed to finish."

He made a grab at the front of Phogor's tunic, and possessed himself of the Venusian's electro-automatic. Congreve subsided.

Fielding had jumped forward again, standing close to Stover. He seemed to dare an assault from the ray-thrower.

"You're convicting yourself, Stover," he charged. "I wanted this will—which has been tampered with—to be heard, and properly witnessed, before the final bands tightened around you. But now—Congreve! This man is armed and desperate, but I know he'll never defeat the law. Before you all, I want to tell what happened earlier tonight."

He pointed a finger at Stover. "He and Captain Sharp accosted me. I took them into my flying machine, intending to turn them over to the police. When we were in the air, and I announced my intention, Stover set off some kind of a bomb. I only escaped because I was strapped in the pilot's seat and had an automatic parachute."

"Certainly you had, since it was you who did the bombing;" Stover shouted him down. "That pilot's seat was the best possible protection, Fielding. It had a high metal back to fend off a blast. The blast itself kicked you loose, seat and all, and the parachute let you down. I escaped by chance and desperation and the luck that wouldn't let a swine like you get away with this dirty string of murders! And there was another figure in the car with us."

"You mean Sharp?" put in Congreve who has been trying to edge in a word for some time.

"No, not Sharp. Someone—something else."

"Preposterous!" snorted Fielding.

Stover turned back to him. "Get back a little, Fielding. I want to look at this bodyguard of yours, the fellow you said you'd hired to protect you from me? Why is he so silent? Why doesn't he get out of the chair?"

When Fielding refused to move, Stover pushed him violently aside. "Look!" he cried to the others.

They looked.

"That's no bodyguard," said Congreve at once. "It isn't a man at all."

"It's nothing alive," put in Amyas Crofts, stepping forward.

"No," said Stover. "Certainly not. Just what is the thing?"

CHAPTER XIX

The Murder Weapon

THEY were all staring now. The draped hulk was not a man. It was a dummy. Its head, rising above the folds of the mantle, was flesh-colored and lifelike, but the full light that now flooded the room showed it up for a painted sham. Its eyes and lips were flat stencil-like blotches, its skin looked taut and puffy.

"It seems to be some sort of hollow shell," commented Stover. "You moved it very easily from chair to chair, Fielding. I wonder if it isn't an inflated shape of thin elascoid—like a toy balloon at a carnival?" He lifted his ray thrower, as though to send a beam at the thing.

"Don't!" Fielding almost screamed.

"Why not?" demanded Stover, and his weapon drew a bead on the lumpy, inflated head. "Why so compassionate over a big air-blown doll? I think I'll just deflate your friend the bodyguard."

His finger seemed to tremble on the trigger-switch of his weapon. Fielding gave another cry, wordless and desperate, and flung himself forward. He caught Stover's wrist, deflecting the aim of the ray thrower.

"You can't do that!" he chattered. "You don't know—you can't know!"

Stover threw him clear, with an effortless jerk of his arm.

"I didn't know," he agreed, "but I'm beginning to find out. Up to now it's been guesswork. Fielding, you've given your show away. If I shot that image—as Malbrook shot the one that was painted to look like me, as poor Gerda slapped the unknown shape that jostled her in the dark closet—or if it received the slightest jar, as the trigger-devices gave to the image of Buckalew at my apartment, and to the dummy in your flying car—it would explode. The detonation would blow us all to bits, including you who figured to explode it if worst came to worst here—but who also figured to escape yourself."

Fielding had recovered himself. He stood between Stover and the dummy.

"I protest at this farce!" he cried to Congreve. "Arrest Stover. If you can't do it alone, deputize these others to overpower and disarm him. I accuse him of tampering with the recorded will of Mace Malbrook and of trying to saddle me with the blame for these dreadful crimes. Probably you'll find, from this additional evidence, that he's definitely the murderer."

"Let me get a word in edgewise," spoke up Reynardine Phogor. "All these recriminations are whizzing by mighty fast, but Fielding is right about one thing. Those last words that came from the television screen weren't in the voice of Mace Malbrook. They were in the voice of Dillon Stover."

"You're right," Stover admitted.

He put away his radium torch and produced another thing from his pocket, a small microphone. "I was near enough to the radio to reach out and switch off the sound track at what I thought was a good moment. And with this mike I substituted my own voice. But I spoiled no will. Fielding had done that already. Look at this."

Reaching into his pocket again, he dug out the ragged coil of film he had found in Malbrook's cupboard.

"Damaged, but partially salvageable. It's Malbrook's true spoken will, undoubtedly cut away from this transcription. Take it, Congreve." And he passed it over.

Phogor was looking into the opened radio mechanism. "Stover has spoken truth. This film has been cut and spliced, a new track worked in."

"Probably Fielding's substituted piece of film is beautifully faked to sound like Malbrook's voice."

"That will," said Fielding, "leaves everything to me."

"It would. That's why you faked it," charged Stover. "Sound laboratories can diagnose and show the truth of all this."

Congreve put away the coil of film. "Everybody's been taking my job out of my hands lately," he growled. "Now I ask, with all the courtesy in the world, to be allowed back into the police business. I pronounce you all under arrest until this is cleared up."

"Let me finish," cried Stover.

"I demand a proper court hearing," Fielding began.

"You'll be heard—and condemned—right here!" Stover said tersely. "This explosive dummy you've brought in among us is the evidence that answers the riddle. A fabric of thin, strong elascoid, made into an airtight form that can be inflated into a very lifelike man. Without air in it, the tube is so slim that it can be inserted into a locked room through as narrow a hole as a ventilator pipe. But the inside's coated with a nitro-glycerin oil, enough to wreck a small area. When inflated from the other side of the hole by a small pump or a tank of compressed air, it becomes a shape that scares the victim, makes him strike or shoot—and brings about his own death."

"You're crazy as well as criminal," raged Fielding.

"You can't prove that fantastic theory."

"But I can," said Stover. "You seemed to be in the clear at Malbrook's because I knocked you down before the explosion. But you'd just finished inflating the elascoid balloon that looked like me. Inside the room, Malbrook saw it and fired. It finished him and poor Prraal."

From his pocket he drew out a shred of elascoid, the bit he had salvaged from the ventilator of the closet where Gerda had died. "Take charge of this, Congreve. It's Exhibit A, a piece of such a figure. I'll explain more fully in a moment."

Again he turned on Fielding. "Most of the fabric of those dummies can be traced as stains—little smears left by the violence of the explosion. And we can examine this one which is still intact. Fielding, you long envied Malbrook his half of the great enterprises you ran together. You long planned this sort of murder—had elascoid dummies ready to finish him and any others you might need to kill.

"When Malbrook decided to fight a duel with me, you struck, figuring I would be found guilty. But you struck too late. For one thing, you found out what Malbrook's will provided. That was why you wanted to marry Reynardine Phogor. When she refused you, you faked the will. Congreve brought us all in to hear it. And you prepared a specimen of your elascoid-and-nitroglycerin handiwork to kill us all if anything went wrong. Instead of which, it's going to convict you!"

"You have proved your point," snarled Fielding without further subterfuge.

Fielding was backing toward the far wall, and in front of him he held the elascoid dummy, divested of its robe. Buckalew, Stover and Congreve pointed their weapons, and Fielding only laughed. "You daren't shoot at my elascoid friend," he warned. "That would dispose of all of us. But I'll take the risk, if you force me."

"By your actions you are confessing, Fielding," said Congreve sharply.

"Yes, and I'm escaping," snarled Fielding. "A few more deaths won't make my punishment any tougher."

"Not after the people you've already killed," agreed Stover. "Better grab him, Congreve, before he cracks."

"How far do you expect to get, Fielding?" demanded Congreve.

"You'll never know. I know Pulambar—hidings, strongholds, disguises. Stand still, all of you. There's a hidden panel, as Stover surmised. If you move before I get through I'll explode my elascoid friend."

Putting a hand behind him, he pressed a stud on the wall. A dark section slid away, revealing a rectangle of darkness.

"Good-by," he taunted them. "Here, now you may have the evidence Mr. Stover so cunningly puzzled out."

And he hurled the inflated figure across the room.

Strover realized later that what followed had been packed into a very brief interval. It was only that his mind was working at rocket-ship speed, outrunning his muscles and reactions, that made everything seem to transpire in slow-motion.

He sprang to catch the elascoid dummy. It was in his thoughts that if someone should die to save the others it might as well be himself who took the explosion against his big body. But somebody else moved more swiftly.

Buckalew!

From the side of the room, Buckalew leaped at an angle. He caught the thing in his arms, and rushed it into the secret passageway by which Fielding was trying to escape. At that instant, the blast came.

Reynardine Phogor screamed, her stepfather caught

and steadied her. Stover and Congreve recovered from the blast of air and pushed their way through the gaping, smoke-filled panel.

The passageway was bulged as to walls and ceiling, but had not sprung apart anywhere. Stover stumbled over the prostrate form of Buckalew, and recovered in time to keep from stepping upon the manifestly dead body of Fielding. Of the dummy remained only another of the elascoid stains.

Stover felt heart-sick as he drew back from Fielding's corpse. Then he heard Buckalew speak.

"I'm all right, Dillon."

As he spoke, Buckalew struggled into a sitting posture. His clothes were in rags, but he smiled cheerfully.

"All right?" repeated Congreve, fumbling around in the passageway. "All right when that nitroglycerin blew a leg off of you?"

He pointed to where it lay, foot, knee and part of the thigh, in a corner. Stover stared miserably. But Buckalew laughed. He drew up the knee he had left, and clasped his arms around it.

"It's not as bad as it looks," he told Congreve gently. "Pick it up and see."

The police investigator did so, gingerly. He uttered a startled exclamation as he dropped the leg in surprise. The limb fell with a metallic clank.

"Artificial!" he snorted, as though this were a prank played deliberately on him. "What next in this space-dizzy case? An artificial leg on a man."

"In a manner of speaking," agreed the victim of the accident. "Stover can help me, Congreve. My leg can be repaired. Don't you think you had better call the coroner for Fielding—and then see about releasing Bee MacGowan right away so she can get in touch with my young friend here?"

Congreve glanced from one to the other and then took a swift look at the body of Brome Fielding. "Yeah," he said a bit sourly. And he stalked out, herding the incoming group back out ahead of him.

Dillon Stover knelt anxiously beside his injured friend. For a few moments the two were alone with only the dead Fielding for company.

"Robert," said Stover, marveling, "you shouldn't have taken such a chance with a—a game leg. I was going to try to capture that dummy and prevent an explosion. And your—your agility amazes me. I've lived intimately with you, and I never dreamed you had an artificial leg."

"Listen, Dillon," said Buckalew in the saddest accents Stover had ever heard him use, "I talked Congreve into going out so I could tell you something that only your grandfather and Malbrook and Fielding knew. I've tried to keep it from you, but you are the one person really entitled to know—and, besides, I need your help now."

"Of course, and you shall have it!" cried Stover vehemently. "I owe you a lot—including my life. Are you sure you aren't injured elsewhere, Robert! Perhaps internally?"

"Only on the surface, Dillon," said Buckalew, smiling faintly. "You don't yet understand. How can a—a thing with an artificial body be injured?"

"But you—*what?*" exclaimed Stover, his blue eyes widening in a startled way as he gazed at the face of the speaker. "What did you say?"

"I have more than one artificial leg, Dillon. I'm a fake through and through—legs, arms, body and head, I am made of metal covered with synthetic rubber flesh. I am the last robot your grandfather made. That's why he gave me the name of Robert."

CHAPTER XX

Table for Three

AGAIN they sat at the Zaarr—Stover, Bee, and Buckalew. It was the same table from which Stover had once risen hotly to smash Malbrook's sneering face.

"Somehow," Stover was saying, "I'm not as shocked as I should be, Buckalew. I think I knew that you were a robot all along."

He gestured at the food and drink served for only two. "This, subconsciously, was my first clue. Yours isn't a normal body, or you'd have to nourish it at times. And then your eternal youth; you knew my grandfather intimately, and you're not a day older now than then. Again, when that explosion happened at our lodgings, you threw yourself in its way and saved me."

"You gave credit for that rescue to the poor robot servitor," reminded Buckalew.

"At first I did. But when you sighed over 'A robot saved you,' you almost gave it away again. Your body, more solidly and strongly made than the metal servitor, kept my beef and bones from being de-atomized. And you didn't pass out on me, but calmly changed clothes."

"Not vanity on my part," Buckalew assured him. "Without clothes I'm pretty evidently an artificial figure. And so I had to think of dressing before I dared awaken you. I dare say I acted very strangely, Dillon, but I was really telling the truth."

"The truth?"

"Fielding magnetized the walls to hold both me and the servitor helpless until you came. Also to hold the inflated copy figure of me up, too, so that when it was released and sagged down the trigger device would set off the explosion. I actually went blank in my mind—it has metal connections, you see. They were frozen inactive until the magnetizing power was turned off. If I was rude or vague, I'm sorry."

"There were more clues," Stover continued. "You didn't fear a shot from Gerda's pistol. You had no sense of dizziness when you climbed down those girders after me; and your body, smaller than mine, was yet heavy enough to pull mine up by the counter-balance of its weight. And—well, won't you tell us the whole story now?"

"Very briefly." Buckalew toyed with the wine glass from which he never drank. "I was made, Dillon, by your grandfather when he was a young man like yourself, studying here. Malbrook's grandfather had engaged him to experiment in robot engineering, and I was the finest example of his work. At first your grandfather was dissatisfied with the sub-mental, sub-personal servitors he evolved—but when he made me, he was heartsick."

"Why?" asked Bee with breathless interest.

Buckalew smiled faintly. "I was a mind, a personality. To him, I was a friend, and a dear friend. But because I was an artificial construction I was property, the property of the man who engaged him." Buckalew was somber. "He stopped making super robots at once, but I was already here. I descended at last to the Malbrook whose death has caused all these curious disclosures."

"So that was his hold over you," summed up Bee.

Buckalew smiled bitterly.

"Yes. He could expose me at any time as an artificial form of life. He could, if he wished, have dismantled and destroyed me. He let me live as if I were a free man, well-supplied with money—but only to run various unpleasant errands for him." Buckalew grew somber, but only for a moment. "I'm free of him now. Nobody knows my real status except the two of you and the heir to Malbrook's property."

"Reynardine Phogor," finished Stover. "Yes, she knows about you."

"What a rotten shame!" put in Bee MacGowan warmly. "She may prove a worse owner than Malbrook."

"I can only find out," sighed Buckalew.

Stover smiled as he signaled a robot waiter, who replenished his glass and Bee's. Then he said: "What were some of your jobs, Robert?"

"The principal one was being Malbrook's financial figurehead. In my name he could speculate. His own operations would have caused too much publicity and set financial opponents on guard against him. With me as a front, he could operate safely. Even if I wanted to cheat or oppose him, I couldn't. He could declare my true status at any time, destroy me, and take my technical holdings. Fielding used me that way, too."

"Could you operate as a financier and business man yourself?" inquired Stover.

Buckalew's artificial eyebrows went up. "Yes. I'm well experienced and adapted. But I'll never get the chance, belonging to Miss Phogor."

"She and I had a conversation while we waited to be interviewed in Congreve's office," said Stover. "First of all, she thought that she owed me everything. Without me, the true bequest to her of the bulk of Malbrook's property would never have been learned. And I agreed very frankly. I asked certain favors."

"About the water rights?"

"Yes, about the water rights," agreed Stover. "They are going to be administered for the good of the whole Martian population—a government project and relief activity, not a money-grubbing monopoly. They'll tide Mars over while the condenser-ray work is being perfected. She agreed that I was right—such things should be. And then I made another stipulation. I asked her for something outright as a reward for my services."

"Reward?" asked Buckalew. "What?"

"You," said Stover succinctly.

For once Buckalew's artificial face betrayed something like mute, human astonishment.

"She made a formal written transfer of her title to you over to me," said Stover. "Technically, you're now my property. That will protect you from any legal trouble as a piece of machinery. But, practically, you belong to yourself."

"To myself," muttered Buckalew. "To myself." He picked up the wineglass. "For the first time since I was made, I wish I could take a drink."

"Come to Earth with me," Stover was urging. "There you'll never be spotted as anything but a man. And you know that Bee and I will never tell on you."

Robert Buckalew looked at him with startled eyes.

"You think I could run my life my own way?"

"Why not? I'll gamble on you. In all of Pulambar, in all of the Solar System, in all of the habitable universe, I could never ask for an animate friend with a braver, warmer, truer heart than you. And here's to your robot health."

Stover and Bee lifted glasses and drank. Buckalew gravely bowed his sleek head.

"Consider a return toast drunk," he said in a voice that for once trembled with the emotion that robots are said never to feel. "We're all safe, all happy, all triumphant. We don't have to fight or hate anyone. Not even Brome Fielding."

"No," agreed Stover. "We can see now that Fielding was beaten from the start."

Both Bee and Buckalew turned sharp gazes upon him.

"How so?" asked Bee. "With Malbrook dead, he was so powerful."

"Exactly," agreed Stover. "It happens that I was sure of his guilt only when I heard that he had possession of that transcribed will. It had been lost. I knew it had been tampered with. So Fielding must have hidden and changed it. The rest of the picture filled itself in. But his position of power was really his downfall. It became more and more evident that a man of supreme power was guilty."

"You started that train of thought when you first said that only one of the High-tower set could have done it," remembered Buckalew.

"Yes. Police secrets, scientific knowledge, a dozen other difficult things, were wielded as weapons by the killer. Even without the evidence that turned up, we could have canceled one suspect after another because of their weaknesses, until we came to the first citizen of Pulambar—Brome Fielding."

Buckalew nodded gravely. "A rationalization worthy of your grandfather, Dillon. You'll start back to work now?"

"Almost at once. I'm going to finish that condenser apparatus, and make Mars fertile again. The Malbrook-Fielding fortune, founded on water monopoly, won't long survive its owners. But," and Stover waved the topic away, "we're celebrating now, aren't we?"

"We are," said Buckalew. "What then? Shall I order a joy-lamp for you two susceptibles?"

Stover turned and looked very fondly at Bee.

"Your eyes are joy-lamp enough," he told her gently, "for me for the rest of my life."

RAMBLE HOUSE's

HARRY STEPHEN KEELER WEBWORK MYSTERIES

(RH) indicates the title is available ONLY in the RAMBLE HOUSE edition

The Ace of Spades Murder
The Affair of the Bottled Deuce (RH)
The Amazing Web
The Barking Clock
Behind That Mask
The Book with the Orange Leaves
The Bottle with the Green Wax Seal
The Box from Japan
The Case of the Canny Killer
The Case of the Crazy Corpse (RH)
The Case of the Flying Hands (RH)
The Case of the Ivory Arrow
The Case of the Jeweled Ragpicker
The Case of the Lavender Gripsack
The Case of the Mysterious Moll
The Case of the 16 Beans
The Case of the Transparent Nude (RH)
The Case of the Transposed Legs
The Case of the Two-Headed Idiot (RH)
The Case of the Two Strange Ladies
The Circus Stealers (RH)
Cleopatra's Tears
A Copy of Beowulf (RH)
The Crimson Cube (RH)
The Face of the Man From Saturn
Find the Clock
The Five Silver Buddhas
The 4th King
The Gallows Waits, My Lord! (RH)
The Green Jade Hand
Finger! Finger!
Hangman's Nights (RH)
I, Chameleon (RH)
I Killed Lincoln at 10:13! (RH)
The Iron Ring
The Man Who Changed His Skin (RH)
The Man with the Crimson Box
The Man with the Magic Eardrums
The Man with the Wooden Spectacles
The Marceau Case
The Matilda Hunter Murder

The Monocled Monster
The Murder of London Lew
The Murdered Mathematician
The Mysterious Card (RH)
The Mysterious Ivory Ball of Wong Shing Li (RH)
The Mystery of the Fiddling Cracksman
The Peacock Fan
The Photo of Lady X (RH)
The Portrait of Jirjohn Cobb
Report on Vanessa Hewstone (RH)
Riddle of the Travelling Skull
Riddle of the Wooden Parrakeet (RH)
The Scarlet Mummy (RH)
The Search for X-Y-Z
The Sharkskin Book
Sing Sing Nights
The Six From Nowhere (RH)
The Skull of the Waltzing Clown
The Spectacles of Mr. Cagliostro
Stand By—London Calling!
The Steeltown Strangler
The Stolen Gravestone (RH)
Strange Journey (RH)
The Strange Will
The Straw Hat Murders (RH)
The Street of 1000 Eyes (RH)
Thieves' Nights
Three Novellos (RH)
The Tiger Snake
The Trap (RH)
Vagabond Nights (Defrauded Yeggman)
Vagabond Nights 2 (10 Hours)
The Vanishing Gold Truck
The Voice of the Seven Sparrows
The Washington Square Enigma
When Thief Meets Thief
The White Circle (RH)
The Wonderful Scheme of Mr. Christo- pher Thorne
X. Jones—of Scotland Yard
Y. Cheung, Business Detective

Keeler Related Works

A To Izzard: A Harry Stephen Keeler Companion by Fender Tucker — Articles and stories about Harry, by Harry, and in his style. Included is a compleat bibliography.

Wild About Harry: Reviews of Keeler Novels — Edited by Richard Polt & Fender Tucker — 22 reviews of works by Harry Stephen Keeler from *Keeler News*. A perfect introduction to the author.

The Keeler Keyhole Collection: Annotated newsletter rants from Harry Stephen Keeler, edited by Francis M. Nevins. Over 400 pages of incredibly personal Keeleriana.

Fakealoo — Pastiches of the style of Harry Stephen Keeler by selected demented members of the HSK Society. Updated every year with the new winner.

Strands of the Web: Short Stories of Harry Stephen Keeler — 29 stories, just about all that Keeler wrote, are edited and introduced by Fred Cleaver.

RAMBLE HOUSE's LOON SANCTUARY

A Clear Path to Cross — Sharon Knowles short mystery stories by Ed Lynskey.

A Corpse Walks in Brooklyn and Other Stories — Volume 5 in the Day Keene in the Detective Pulps series.

A Jimmy Starr Omnibus — Three 40s novels by Jimmy Starr.

A Niche in Time and Other Stories — Classic SF by William F. Temple

A Roland Daniel Double: The Signal and The Return of Wu Fang — Classic thrillers from the 30s.

A Shot Rang Out — Three decades of reviews and articles by today's Anthony Boucher, Jon Breen. An essential book for any mystery lover's library.

A Smell of Smoke — A 1951 English countryside thriller by Miles Burton.

A Snark Selection — Lewis Carroll's *The Hunting of the Snark* with two Snarkian chapters by Harry Stephen Keeler — Illustrated by Gavin L. O'Keefe.

A Young Man's Heart — A forgotten early classic by Cornell Woolrich.

Alexander Laing Novels — *The Motives of Nicholas Holtz* and *Dr. Scarlett*, stories of medical mayhem and intrigue from the 30s.

An Angel in the Street — Modern hardboiled noir by Peter Genovese.

Automaton — Brilliant treatise on robotics: 1928-style! By H. Stafford Hatfield.

Away From the Here and Now — Clare Winger Harris stories, collected by Richard A. Lupoff.

Beast or Man? — A 1930 novel of racism and horror by Sean M'Guire. Introduced by John Pelan.

Black Beadle — A 1939 thriller by E.C.R. Lorac.

Black Hogan Strikes Again — Australia's Peter Renwick pens a tale of the 30s outback.

Black River Falls — Suspense from the master, Ed Gorman.

Blondy's Boy Friend — A snappy 1930 story by Philip Wylie, writing as Leatrice Homesley.

Blood in a Snap — The *Finnegan's Wake* of the 21st century, by Jim Weiler.

Blood Moon — The first of the Robert Payne series by Ed Gorman.

Bogart '48 — Hollywood action with Bogie by John Stanley and Kenn Davis

Calling Lou Largo! — Two Lou Largo novels by William Ard.

Cornucopia of Crime — Francis M. Nevins assembled this huge collection of his writings about crime literature and the people who write it. Essential for any serious mystery library.

Corpse Without Flesh — Strange novel of forensics by George Bruce

Crimson Clown Novels — By Johnston McCulley, author of the Zorro novels, *The Crimson Clown* and *The Crimson Clown Again*.

Dago Red — 22 tales of dark suspense by Bill Pronzini.

Dark Sanctuary — Weird Menace story by H. B. Gregory

David Hume Novels — *Corpses Never Argue, Cemetery First Stop, Make Way for the Mourners, Eternity Here I Come*. 1930s British hardboiled fiction with an attitude.

Dead Man Talks Too Much — Hollywood boozer by Weed Dickenson.

Death Leaves No Card — One of the most unusual murdered-in-the-tub mysteries you'll ever read. By Miles Burton.

Death March of the Dancing Dolls and Other Stories — Volume Three in the Day Keene in the Detective Pulps series. Introduced by Bill Crider.

Deep Space and other Stories — A collection of SF gems by Richard A. Lupoff.

Detective Duff Unravels It — Episodic mysteries by Harvey O'Higgins.

Diabolic Candelabra — Classic 30s mystery by E.R. Punshon

Dictator's Way — Another D.S. Bobby Owen mystery from E.R. Punshon

Dime Novels: Ramble House's 10-Cent Books — *Knife in the Dark* by Robert Leslie Bellem, *Hot Lead* and *Song of Death* by Ed Earl Repp, *A Hashish House in New York* by H.H. Kane, and five more.

Doctor Arnoldi — Tiffany Thayer's story of the death of death.

Don Diablo: Book of a Lost Film — Two-volume treatment of a western by Paul Landres, with diagrams. Intro by Francis M. Nevins.

Dope and Swastikas — Two strange novels from 1922 by Edmund Snell

Dope Tales #1 — Two dope-riddled classics; *Dope Runners* by Gerald Grantham and *Death Takes the Joystick* by Phillip Condé.

Dope Tales #2 — Two more narco-classics; *The Invisible Hand* by Rex Dark and *The Smokers of Hashish* by Norman Berrow.

Dope Tales #3 — Two enchanting novels of opium by the master, Sax Rohmer. *Dope* and *The Yellow Claw.*

Double Hot — Two 60s softcore sex novels by Morris Hershman.

Double Sex — Yet two more panting thrillers from Morris Hershman.

Dr. Odin — Douglas Newton's 1933 racial potboiler comes back to life.

Evangelical Cockroach — Jack Woodford writes about writing.

Evidence in Blue — 1938 mystery by E. Charles Vivian.

Fatal Accident — Murder by automobile, a 1936 mystery by Cecil M. Wills.

Fighting Mad — Todd Robbins' 1922 novel about boxing and life

Finger-prints Never Lie — A 1939 classic detective novel by John G. Brandon.

Freaks and Fantasies — Eerie tales by Tod Robbins, collaborator of Tod Browning on the film FREAKS.

Gadsby — A lipogram (a novel without the letter E). Ernest Vincent Wright's last work, published in 1939 right before his death.

Gelett Burgess Novels — *The Master of Mysteries, The White Cat, Two O'Clock Courage, Ladies in Boxes, Find the Woman, The Heart Line, The Picaroons* and *Lady Mechante.* Recently added is A Gelett Burgess Sampler, edited by Alfred Jan. All are introduced by Richard A. Lupoff.

Geronimo — S. M. Barrett's 1905 autobiography of a noble American.

Hake Talbot Novels — *Rim of the Pit, The Hangman's Handyman.* Classic locked room mysteries, with mapback covers by Gavin O'Keefe.

Hands Out of Hell and Other Stories — John H. Knox's eerie hallucinations

Hell is a City — William Ard's masterpiece.

Hollywood Dreams — A novel of Tinsel Town and the Depression by Richard O'Brien.

Hostesses in Hell and Other Stories — Russell Gray's most graphic stories

House of the Restless Dead — Strange and ominous tales by Hugh B. Cave

I Stole $16,000,000 — A true story by cracksman Herbert E. Wilson.

Inclination to Murder — 1966 thriller by New Zealand's Harriet Hunter.

Invaders from the Dark — Classic werewolf tale from Greye La Spina.

J. Poindexter, Colored — Classic satirical black novel by Irvin S. Cobb.

Jack Mann Novels — Strange murder in the English countryside. *Gees' First Case, Nightmare Farm, Grey Shapes, The Ninth Life, The Glass Too Many, Her Ways Are Death, The Kleinert Case* and *Maker of Shadows.*

Jake Hardy — A lusty western tale from Wesley Tallant.

Jim Harmon Double Novels — *Vixen Hollow/Celluloid Scandal, The Man Who Made Maniacs/Silent Siren, Ape Rape/Wanton Witch, Sex Burns Like Fire/Twist Session, Sudden Lust/Passion Strip, Sin Unlimited/Harlot Master, Twilight Girls/Sex Institution.* Written in the early 60s and never reprinted until now.

Joel Townsley Rogers Novels and Short Stories — By the author of *The Red Right Hand: Once In a Red Moon, Lady With the Dice, The Stopped Clock, Never Leave My Bed.* Also two short story collections: *Night of Horror* and *Killing Time.*

John Carstairs, Space Detective — Arboreal Sci-fi by Frank Belknap Long

Joseph Shallit Novels — *The Case of the Billion Dollar Body, Lady Don't Die on My Doorstep, Kiss the Killer, Yell Bloody Murder, Take Your Last Look.* One of America's best 50's authors and a favorite of author Bill Pronzini.

Keller Memento — 45 short stories of the amazing and weird by Dr. David Keller.

Killer's Caress — Cary Moran's 1936 hardboiled thriller.

Lady of the Yellow Death and Other Stories — More stories by Wyatt Blassingame.

League of the Grateful Dead and Other Stories — Volume One in the Day Keene in the Detective Pulps series.

Library of Death — Ghastly tale by Ronald S. L. Harding, introduced by John Pelan.

Malcolm Jameson Novels and Short Stories — *Astonishing! Astounding!, Tarnished Bomb, The Alien Envoy and Other Stories* and *The Chariots of San Fernando and Other Stories.* All introduced and edited by John Pelan or Richard A. Lupoff.

Man Out of Hell and Other Stories — Volume II of the John H. Knox weird pulps collection.

Marblehead: A Novel of H.P. Lovecraft — A long-lost masterpiece from Richard A. Lupoff. This is the "director's cut", the long version that has never been published before.

Mark of the Laughing Death and Other Stories — Shockers from the pulps by Francis James, introduced by John Pelan.

Master of Souls — Mark Hansom's 1937 shocker is introduced by weirdologist John Pelan.

Max Afford Novels — *Owl of Darkness, Death's Mannikins, Blood on His Hands, The Dead Are Blind, The Sheep and the Wolves, Sinners in Paradise* and *Two Locked Room Mysteries and a Ripping Yarn* by one of Australia's finest mystery novelists.

Money Brawl — Two books about the writing business by Jack Woodford and H. Bedford-Jones. Introduced by Richard A. Lupoff.

More Secret Adventures of Sherlock Holmes — Gary Lovisi's second collection of tales about the unknown sides of the great detective.

Muddled Mind: Complete Works of Ed Wood, Jr. — David Hayes and Hayden Davis deconstruct the life and works of the mad, but canny, genius.

Murder among the Nudists — A mystery from 1934 by Peter Hunt, featuring a naked Detective-Inspector going undercover in a nudist colony.

Murder in Black and White — 1931 classic tennis whodunit by Evelyn Elder.

Murder in Shawnee — Two novels of the Alleghenies by John Douglas: *Shawnee Alley Fire* and *Haunts.*

Murder in Silk — A 1937 Yellow Peril novel of the silk trade by Ralph Trevor.

My Deadly Angel — 1955 Cold War drama by John Chelton.

My First Time: The One Experience You Never Forget — Michael Birchwood — 64 true first-person narratives of how they lost it.

Mysterious Martin, the Master of Murder — Two versions of a strange 1912 novel by Tod Robbins about a man who writes books that can kill.

Norman Berrow Novels — *The Bishop's Sword, Ghost House, Don't Go Out After Dark, Claws of the Cougar, The Smokers of Hashish, The Secret Dancer, Don't Jump Mr. Boland!, The Footprints of Satan, Fingers for Ransom, The Three Tiers of Fantasy, The Spaniard's Thumb, The Eleventh Plague, Words Have Wings, One Thrilling Night, The Lady's in Danger, It Howls at Night, The Terror in the Fog, Oil Under the Window, Murder in the Melody, The Singing Room.* This is the complete Norman Berrow library of locked-room mysteries, several of which are masterpieces.

Old Faithful and Other Stories — SF classic tales by Raymond Z. Gallun

Old Times' Sake — Short stories by James Reasoner from Mike Shayne Magazine.

One Dreadful Night — A classic mystery by Ronald S. L. Harding

Pair O' Jacks — A mystery novel and a diatribe about publishing by Jack Woodford

Perfect .38 — Two early Timothy Dane novels by William Ard. More to come.

Prince Pax — Devilish intrigue by George Sylvester Viereck and Philip Eldridge

Prose Bowl — Futuristic satire of a world where hack writing has replaced football as our national obsession, by Bill Pronzini and Barry N. Malzberg.

Red Light — The history of legal prostitution in Shreveport Louisiana by Eric Brock. Includes wonderful photos of the houses and the ladies.

Researching American-Made Toy Soldiers — A 276-page collection of a lifetime of articles by toy soldier expert Richard O'Brien.

Reunion in Hell — Volume One of the John H. Knox series of weird stories from the pulps. Introduced by horror expert John Pelan.

Ripped from the Headlines! — The Jack the Ripper story as told in the newspaper articles in the *New York* and *London Times.*

Rough Cut & New, Improved Murder — Ed Gorman's first two novels.

R.R. Ryan Novels — Freak Museum and The Subjugated Beast, two horror classics.

Ruby of a Thousand Dreams — The villain Wu Fang returns in this Roland Daniel novel.

Ruled By Radio — 1925 futuristic novel by Robert L. Hadfield & Frank E. Farncombe.

Rupert Penny Novels — *Policeman's Holiday, Policeman's Evidence, Lucky Policeman, Policeman in Armour, Sealed Room Murder, Sweet Poison, The Talkative Policeman, She had to Have Gas* and *Cut and Run* (by Martin Tanner.) Rupert Penny is the pseudonym of Australian Charles Thornett, a master of the locked room, impossible crime plot.

Sacred Locomotive Flies — Richard A. Lupoff's psychedelic SF story.

Sam — Early gay novel by Lonnie Coleman.

Sand's Game — Spectacular hard-boiled noir from Ennis Willie, edited by Lynn Myers and Stephen Mertz, with contributions from Max Allan Collins, Bill Crider, Wayne Dundee, Bill Pronzini, Gary Lovisi and James Reasoner.

Sand's War — More violent fiction from the typewriter of Ennis Willie

Satan's Den Exposed — True crime in Truth or Consequences New Mexico — Award-winning journalism by the *Desert Journal*.

Satans of Saturn — Novellas from the pulps by Otis Adelbert Kline and E. H. Price

Satan's Sin House and Other Stories — Horrific gore by Wayne Rogers

Secrets of a Teenage Superhero — Graphic lit by Jonathan Sweet

Sex Slave — Potboiler of lust in the days of Cleopatra by Dion Leclerq, 1966.

Sideslip — 1968 SF masterpiece by Ted White and Dave Van Arnam.

Slammer Days — Two full-length prison memoirs: *Men into Beasts* (1952) by George Sylvester Viereck and *Home Away From Home* (1962) by Jack Woodford.

Slippery Staircase — 1930s whodunit from E.C.R. Lorac.

Sorcerer's Chessmen — John Pelan introduces this 1939 classic by Mark Hansom.

Star Griffin — Michael Kurland's 1987 masterpiece of SF drollery is back.

Stakeout on Millennium Drive — Award-winning Indianapolis Noir by Ian Woollen.

Strands of the Web: Short Stories of Harry Stephen Keeler — Edited and Introduced by Fred Cleaver.

Summer Camp for Corpses and Other Stories — Weird Menace tales from Arthur Leo Zagat; introduced by John Pelan.

Suzy — A collection of comic strips by Richard O'Brien and Bob Vojtko from 1970.

Tales of the Macabre and Ordinary — Modern twisted horror by Chris Mikul, author of the *Bizarrism* series.

Tales of Terror and Torment #1 — John Pelan selects and introduces this sampler of weird menace tales from the pulps.

Tenebrae — Ernest G. Henham's 1898 horror tale brought back.

The Amorous Intrigues & Adventures of Aaron Burr — by Anonymous. Hot historical action about the man who almost became Emperor of Mexico.

The Anthony Boucher Chronicles — edited by Francis M. Nevins. Book reviews by Anthony Boucher written for the *San Francisco Chronicle*, 1942 – 1947. Essential and fascinating reading by the best book reviewer there ever was.

The Barclay Catalogs — Two essential books about toy soldier collecting by Richard O'Brien

The Basil Wells Omnibus — A collection of Wells' stories by Richard A. Lupoff

The Beautiful Dead and Other Stories — Dreadful tales from Donald Dale

The Best of 10-Story Book — edited by Chris Mikul, over 35 stories from the literary magazine Harry Stephen Keeler edited.

The Black Dark Murders — Vintage 50s college murder yarn by Milt Ozaki, writing as Robert O. Saber.

The Book of Time — The classic novel by H.G. Wells is joined by sequels by Wells himself and three stories by Richard A. Lupoff. Illustrated by Gavin L. O'Keefe.

The Case in the Clinic — One of E.C.R. Lorac's finest.

The Strange Case of the Antlered Man — A mystery of superstition by Edwy Searles Brooks.

The Case of the Bearded Bride — #4 in the Day Keene in the Detective Pulps series

The Case of the Little Green Men — Mack Reynolds wrote this love song to sci-fi fans back in 1951 and it's now back in print.

The Case of the Withered Hand — 1936 potboiler by John G. Brandon.

The Charlie Chaplin Murder Mystery — A 2004 tribute by noted film scholar, Wes D. Gehring.

The Chinese Jar Mystery — Murder in the manor by John Stephen Strange, 1934.

The Cloudbuilders and Other Stories — SF tales from Colin Kapp.

The Compleat Calhoon — All of Fender Tucker's works: Includes *Totah Six-Pack, Weed, Women and Song* and *Tales from the Tower,* plus a CD of all of his songs.

The Compleat Ova Hamlet — Parodies of SF authors by Richard A. Lupoff. This is a brand new edition with more stories and more illustrations by Trina Robbins.

The Contested Earth and Other SF Stories — A never-before published space opera and seven short stories by Jim Harmon.

The Crimson Query — A 1929 thriller from Arlton Eadie. A perfect way to get introduced.

The Curse of Cantire — Classic 1939 novel of a family curse by Walter S. Masterman.

The Devil and the C.I.D. — Odd diabolic mystery by E.C.R. Lorac

The Devil Drives — An odd prison and lost treasure novel from 1932 by Virgil Markham.

The Devil of Pei-Ling — Herbert Asbury's 1929 tale of the occult.

The Devil's Mistress — A 1915 Scottish gothic tale by J. W. Brodie-Innes, a member of Aleister Crowley's Golden Dawn.

The Devil's Nightclub and Other Stories — John Pelan introduces some gruesome tales by Nat Schachner.

The Disentanglers — Episodic intrigue at the turn of last century by Andrew Lang

The Dog Poker Code — A spoof of *The Da Vinci Code* by D.B. Smithee.

The Dumpling — Political murder from 1907 by Coulson Kernahan.

The End of It All and Other Stories — Ed Gorman selected his favorite short stories for this huge collection.

The Fangs of Suet Pudding — A 1944 novel of the German invasion by Adams Farr

The Finger of Destiny and Other Stories — Edmund Snell's superb collection of weird stories of Borneo.

The Ghost of Gaston Revere — From 1935, a novel of life and beyond by Mark Hansom, introduced by John Pelan.

The Girl in the Dark — A thriller from Roland Daniel

The Gold Star Line — Seaboard adventure from L.T. Reade and Robert Eustace.

The Golden Dagger — 1951 Scotland Yard yarn by E. R. Punshon.

The Great Orme Terror — Horror stories by Garnett Radcliffe from the pulps

The Hairbreadth Escapes of Major Mendax — Francis Blake Crofton's 1889 boys' book.

The House That Time Forgot and Other Stories — Insane pulpitude by Robert F. Young

The House of the Vampire — 1907 poetic thriller by George S. Viereck.

The Illustrious Corpse — Murder hijinx from Tiffany Thayer

The Incredible Adventures of Rowland Hern — Intriguing 1928 impossible crimes by Nicholas Olde.

The Julius Caesar Murder Case — A classic 1935 re-telling of the assassination by Wallace Irwin that's much more fun than the Shakespeare version.

The Koky Comics — A collection of all of the 1978-1981 Sunday and daily comic strips by Richard O'Brien and Mort Gerberg, in two volumes.

The Lady of the Terraces — 1925 missing race adventure by E. Charles Vivian.

The Lord of Terror — 1925 mystery with master-criminal, Fantômas.

The Melamare Mystery — A classic 1929 Arsene Lupin mystery by Maurice Leblanc

The Man Who Was Secrett — Epic SF stories from John Brunner

The Man Without a Planet — Science fiction tales by Richard Wilson

The N. R. De Mexico Novels — Robert Bragg, the real N.R. de Mexico, presents *Marijuana Girl, Madman on a Drum, Private Chauffeur* in one volume.

The Night Remembers — A 1991 Jack Walsh mystery from Ed Gorman.

The One After Snelling — Kickass modern noir from Richard O'Brien.

The Organ Reader — A huge compilation of just about everything published in the 1971-1972 radical bay-area newspaper, *THE ORGAN*. A coffee table book that points out the shallowness of the coffee table mindset.

The Poker Club — Three in one! Ed Gorman's ground-breaking novel, the short story it was based upon, and the screenplay of the film made from it.

The Private Journal & Diary of John H. Surratt — The memoirs of the man who conspired to assassinate President Lincoln.

The Ramble House Mapbacks — Recently revised book by Gavin L. O'Keefe with color pictures of all the Ramble House books with mapbacks.

The Secret Adventures of Sherlock Holmes — Three Sherlockian pastiches by the Brooklyn author/publisher, Gary Lovisi.

The Shadow on the House — Mark Hansom's 1934 masterpiece of horror is introduced by John Pelan.

The Sign of the Scorpion — A 1935 Edmund Snell tale of oriental evil.

The Singular Problem of the Stygian House-Boat — Two classic tales by John Kendrick Bangs about the denizens of Hades.

The Smiling Corpse — Philip Wylie and Bernard Bergman's odd 1935 novel.

The Spider: Satan's Murder Machines — A thesis about Iron Man

The Stench of Death: An Odoriferous Omnibus by Jack Moskovitz — Two complete novels and two novellas from 60's sleaze author, Jack Moskovitz.

The Story Writer and Other Stories — Classic SF from Richard Wilson

The Strange Case of the Antlered Man — 1935 dementia from Edwy Searles Brooks

The Strange Thirteen — Richard B. Gamon's odd stories about Raj India.

The Technique of the Mystery Story — Carolyn Wells' tips about writing.

The Threat of Nostalgia — A collection of his most obscure stories by Jon Breen

The Time Armada — Fox B. Holden's 1953 SF gem.

The Tongueless Horror and Other Stories — Volume One of the series of short stories from the weird pulps by Wyatt Blassingame.

The Town from Planet Five — From Richard Wilson, two SF classics, *And Then the Town Took Off* and *The Girls from Planet 5*

The Tracer of Lost Persons — From 1906, an episodic novel that became a hit radio series in the 30s. Introduced by Richard A. Lupoff.

The Trail of the Cloven Hoof — Diabolical horror from 1935 by Arlton Eadie. Introduced by John Pelan.

The Triune Man — Mindscrambling science fiction from Richard A. Lupoff.

The Unholy Goddess and Other Stories — Wyatt Blassingame's first DTP compilation

The Universal Holmes — Richard A. Lupoff's 2007 collection of five Holmesian pastiches and a recipe for giant rat stew.

The Werewolf vs the Vampire Woman — Hard to believe ultraviolence by either Arthur M. Scarm or Arthur M. Scram.

The Whistling Ancestors — A 1936 classic of weirdness by Richard E. Goddard and introduced by John Pelan.

The White Owl — A vintage thriller from Edmund Snell

The White Peril in the Far East — Sidney Lewis Gulick's 1905 indictment of the West and assurance that Japan would never attack the U.S.

The Wizard of Berner's Abbey — A 1935 horror gem written by Mark Hansom and introduced by John Pelan.

The Wonderful Wizard of Oz — by L. Frank Baum and illustrated by Gavin L. O'Keefe.

Through the Looking Glass — Lewis Carroll wrote it; Gavin L. O'Keefe illustrated it.

Time Line — Ramble House artist Gavin O'Keefe selects his most evocative art inspired by the twisted literature he reads and designs.

Tiresias — Psychotic modern horror novel by Jonathan M. Sweet.

Tortures and Towers — Two novellas of terror by Dexter Dayle.

Totah Six-Pack — Fender Tucker's six tales about Farmington in one sleek volume.

Tree of Life, Book of Death — Grania Davis' book of her life.

Triple Quest — An arty mystery from the 30s by E.R. Punshon.

Trail of the Spirit Warrior — Roger Haley's saga of life in the Indian Territories.

Two Kinds of Bad — Two 50s novels by William Ard about Danny Fontaine

Two Suns of Morcali and Other Stories — Evelyn E. Smith's SF tour-de-force

Ultra-Boiled — 23 gut-wrenching tales by our Man in Brooklyn, Gary Lovisi.

Up Front From Behind — A 2011 satire of Wall Street by James B. Kobak.

Victims & Villains — Intriguing Sherlockiana from Derham Groves.

Wade Wright Novels — *Echo of Fear, Death At Nostalgia Street, It Leads to Murder* and *Shadows' Edge*, a double book featuring *Shadows Don't Bleed* and *The Sharp Edge*.

Walter S. Masterman Novels — *The Green Toad, The Flying Beast, The Yellow Mistletoe, The Wrong Verdict, The Perjured Alibi, The Border Line, The Bloodhounds Bay, The Curse of Cantire* and *The Baddington Horror*. Masterman wrote horror and mystery, some introduced by John Pelan.

We Are the Dead and Other Stories — Volume Two in the Day Keene in the Detective Pulps series, introduced by Ed Gorman. When done, there may be 11 in the series.

Welsh Rarebit Tales — Charming stories from 1902 by Harle Oren Cummins

West Texas War and Other Western Stories — by Gary Lovisi.

What If? Volume 1, 2 and 3 — Richard A. Lupoff introduces three decades worth of SF short stories that should have won a Hugo, but didn't.

When the Batman Thirsts and Other Stories — Weird tales from Frederick C. Davis.

Whip Dodge: Man Hunter — Wesley Tallant's saga of a bounty hunter of the old West.

Win, Place and Die! — The first new mystery by Milt Ozaki in decades. The ultimate novel of 70s Reno.

Writer 1 and 2 — A magnus opus from Richard A. Lupoff summing up his life as writer.

You'll Die Laughing — Bruce Elliott's 1945 novel of murder at a practical joker's English countryside manor.

RAMBLE HOUSE

Fender Tucker, Prop.   Gavin L. O'Keefe, Graphics
www.ramblehouse.com   fender@ramblehouse.com
228-826-1783   10329 Sheephead Drive, Vancleave MS 39565